FIREWEATHER

FIREWEATHER
MIRANDA DARLING

SCRIBE

Melbourne | London | Minneapolis

Scribe Publications
18–20 Edward St, Brunswick, Victoria 3056, Australia
2 John St, Clerkenwell, London, WC1N 2ES, United Kingdom
3754 Pleasant Ave, Suite 223w, Minneapolis, Minnesota 55409, USA

Published by Scribe 2025

Copyright © Miranda Darling 2025

The publisher expressly prohibits the use of *Fireweather* in connection with the development of any software program, including, without limitation, training a machine-learning or generative artificial intelligence (AI) system.

All rights reserved, including those for text and data mining, AI training, and similar technologies. Without limiting the rights under copyright reserved above, no part of this publication may be reproduced, stored in or introduced into a retrieval system, or transmitted, in any form or by any means (electronic, mechanical, photocopying, recording or otherwise) without the prior written permission of the publishers of this book.

The moral rights of the author have been asserted.

Typeset in Garamond by Duncan Blachford, Typography Studio

Printed and bound in the UK by CPI Group (UK) Ltd, Croydon CR0 4YY

Scribe is committed to the sustainable use of natural resources and the use of paper products made responsibly from those resources.

978 1 761381 37 9 (Australian edition)
978 1 917189 04 0 (UK edition)
978 1 964992 22 8 (US edition)

Catalogue records for this book are available from the National Library of Australia and the British Library.

scribepublications.com.au
scribepublications.co.uk
scribepublications.com

Dedicated to the Endangered and the Vanishing Ones

What the caterpillar calls catastrophe,
the master calls butterfly.

It all began with the bird.
It all began with the fire.
It all began with the plant.
It all began when they started running away.
Also, this is a love story.

THE BRAIN SCAN: MORNING

NO, IT ISN'T GOING to hurt, the technician assures me.

'We're just going to stress your brain.'

'Okay.'

How will that be different?

The technician is a lovely woman who introduces herself as Parvati and explains patiently that evidence is being sought for a faulty brain. The word 'tumour' is skirted carefully, but the shadow its absence casts into the conversation throws it off kilter, and We Both Know. Temporal lobe seizures ...? Epilepsy, perhaps?

(If we break apart the word chains then different thoughtforms become possible — like molecular chains, so our symbols of language)

See Apocalypse:

'/ /o\o c|o/ '\|o () c-

And Madness?

/ '_/ o | o_/ '(| '< {{

I feel it prudent not to draw that word into the room either: twin shadows, then.

Parvati will be creating stimuli to provoke my brain into seizing or otherwise behaving abnormally. This will involve noise, flashing lights, and so on. Electrodes will be attached to my skull with globs of sticky wax. This, too, will be painless.

I sit up straight and submit to her touch on my head, a child to her mother's fingers, braiding her hair. The technician has a calming effect on me. I imagine how good it must feel to be Parvati: to have her supple, slender, purposeful limbs, her dark braid, expertly plaited, her spectacles. I glimpse a perfect little lunch box in her tidy tote, sitting by the door. Parvati is calm and intelligent and helpful, and I am sure she would know exactly, at every point in her day, where her feet should be placed.

She turns off the lights and retreats to an illuminated box on the far wall.

Would this ever end, this testing and compiling and checking and assessing? Before All This (and I include some of the first half of my marriage as Before) I was the sort of person who went to the doctor once a year, and that was usually for a vaccination for travel somewhere remote, or for a sliced finger needing stitches.

Check-ups became regular during and right after my pregnancies, but they were pragmatic, (for me, fortunately) largely untroublesome, and joyful. I went to all my appointments alone, but I didn't mind that. He was very busy, and these baby appointments were something I could manage by myself. We would discuss the results later at home: I would show ultrasounds or explain cervical strength; He would ring the obstetrician — a friend of His — and confirm what I had told him. I learned to breathe calmly. He breathed with me; that was something we could do together.

Seeing the very first ultrasound of my grain of rice with a heartbeat like a whale hit me with shock and wonder, with a wave of love that has yet to leave me, that never will.

I floated in this state of delicious anticipation — the Italian phrase for it is dolce attesa, the 'sweet waiting', which strikes me as a far more romantic and beautiful notion than 'pregnancy term' — until my contractions started nine weeks too early. Then all was management, and a taut, humming concern sang along undersea cables, twanged, hummed subsonic. I did everything exactly as I was told; I did everything I could to keep my baby inside for as long as I could. I learnt then my first great lesson of surrender: there are so many things you cannot fight against — in fact, many of them grow stronger if you do fight; so many things that you must cede to, gracefully or not: a swelling body, muscles spasming and contracting so hard, so ineluctably, that there is no choice but to cede all will to the giant invisible hand that is crushing your insides. I surrendered to steroid injections into the balloon of my belly, and the idea that I could not hold my baby inside me through sheer will or grit; I surrendered to an eventual birth that took four days and had me vomiting with pain.

I held my baby, born so small he weighed two-and-a-half blocks of butter. I surrendered to the eternal patience of pumping milk every three hours into a feeding tube to his nose and trying to teach him to suck, to get him strong enough to feed on his own. I learnt that hospitals cannot have you stay with your baby more than a few nights, and I surrendered to leaving him in Special Care for four weeks. I drove myself there every day for the 6 am feed and did not leave until after 9 pm. Each time I drove away from the hospital, my womb started cramping, my breasts filled, my eyes filled with tears. My baby was still part of my body.

I napped in the feeding room and ate Anzac biscuits with the nurses who taught me how to care for my baby with such kindness; I embroidered muslin cloths — with no skill but all the love in the world — by his crib as he slept, watching the monitor attached to his foot pound its small steady rhythm and picking out ducklings in yellow thread.

I willed my entire being into my tiny son, to make him okay. I surrendered to Him bringing streams of visitors, two by two, into the nursery, bringing men I did not trust or even like to watch me struggle to breastfeed. I spun a protective cocoon around my baby and me, and shut out the world.

I surrendered to a force far greater than Him, or hospitals; I surrendered utterly and completely to Love. Real Love. I surrendered to the utter vulnerability that comes with it. Nothing has been the same since.

My brain kaleidoscopes, and the inner voices slip out between the moving pieces to have their say. I have nicknamed them so it's easier to keep track of the conversations in my mind, but they are no less insistent for it. Some voices are more helpful than others, but none will be silenced easily.

THE POET: The Queendom of your love has been a provocation to the delusions of wealth, of self, to the violent arrogance of physical power. You have destabilised a pillar of this world and this world is resisting.

(The Poet is a little florid, but her language is tolerable because occasionally her insights get to the heart of the matter; The Nanny is pragmatic to the point of bossy and she almost always has something to say.)

THE NANNY: This world is about to electrocute your head!

It's just to establish —

THE ARCHER: If you could only see yourself. You look freakish. You look absolutely mad.

(And, of course, The Archer — always the snide take, always

hitting a bullseye in my psyche, but I can't ignore them. The Archer keeps me safe.)

In that dark room, on the hard plastic chair, I shake myself and draw down thoughts like kites. It is important to retain some cohesion when dealing with these matters.

'Shall we begin?' Parvati speaks through a microphone. I see her reassuring smile from the lit box, Mission Control to my Laika.

I nod and return her smile, picturing every horrific asylum electroshock-therapy scene from every film I have ever watched.

Strobe lights, noises like machine guns, bursts, flashes, booming — all designed to see how your brain responds to distressing elements. I allow the sensorial provocation to break over my head like so many eggs; I keep my mind blank and still. Parvati's experiments do not upset my equilibrium. My physical brain is as steady as a rock.

At the end, Parvati explains that she cannot tell me the results, as she is not a doctor. But we have enjoyed each other's company, been equal participants in this strange experiment — I have been respectful of her skill, and she has been careful to explain the process to me (this is not always the case) — and she seems to relent as she begins tugging the electrodes out of my hair:

'You don't have epilepsy.'

I nod. Remind myself that this is a Good Thing. A Good Thing that, however, leaves a chasm of the Unknown still yawning.

'And there is no sinister mass.'

She pauses, so I can understand what she is referring to.

Ah.

'That's a ... relief.' But the other question remains. 'So, why?'

'Anybody can be induced to have seizures if the conditions are right.'

The wax is sticky and all through my hair now. I'm glad I brought a brush and an elastic to tie my hair up when I leave the hospital.

'Dehydration, altitude, extreme emotional distress ... these can all trigger seizures in a healthy brain.'

Parvati stops what she is doing, and we pause again to absorb this. My eyes feel huge in the dark room. The questions — hers and mine — gather like constellations, but we leave them unasked. If we draw down one star, we risk pulling down the heavens.

'You will have to see a neurologist.' She breaks the moment, bundling the electrodes with her efficient fingers. 'But I really don't think there is anything to worry about.'

(And you can't drive for six months.)

What I say to Parvati:

'Goodbye. Thank you for all your help today. I really appreciate your patience and skill.'

What I don't say to Parvati:

'Dark matter can only be studied by measuring the consequence of its presence.'

I HAVE BEGUN RHYMING words like rosary beads, like litanies — when my mind is particularly anxious, it casts about uncontrollably for associative sounds. I don't know if this is a form of Tourette's or something obsessive-compulsive; I only know it is quite new, and I'm glad it only happens in my head and not out loud. It's both nonsense and an early warning system, a reminder that many things sound the same but are not alike at all. Words join others until they circle my mind like a wall of barracuda, shining silver, moving as one, and I am beneath them, looking up, and below and above is Deep Blue. I experience a sort of rapture of the deep, like nitrogen narcosis when diving, brought on by breathing compressed inert gases and manifesting in a change in consciousness and neuromuscular function — irrationality, visions, disorientation.

Blue fever.

The first time it happened is a clear memory: I am in the park and the children are climbing the shoulders of an enormous Moreton Bay — a motherfig; it is the afternoon of the first time they ran away. (They took a bus from school alone together and turned up at the front door, eyes wide with the terror of what they had done.) I have sent a message to let their father know they are safe, that they are with me. He calls, and I pick up because I have not yet learned that this is something I should never do.

The voice is icy with fury. It orders me to bring the children. They are on His time, it is His right. I tell Him the children are upset, they don't want to go today. They need a little time. I am pleading now, really pleading.

'Let them spend the night with me and I'll bring them back tomorrow morning—'

The control breaks then, and the shouting starts, the repetition of aggressive phrases flooding over my words. I refuse to tell Him where we are. The boys are safe, I repeat — name, rank, serial number — as if saying it enough times will make it so. I find all my courage and tell Him He has to be kinder — He can't behave that way towards them, they are children, they are frightened — He explodes with rage. I hold the phone a little further from my ear.

He tells me no one will ever believe anything I say because I am mentally ill — everyone knows!! — and He can prove it.

'I am not mentally ill.' I say it. My throat swells, trembles with anger, with fear, with the terror-thrill audacity of my resistance, but I fight to keep the emotion out of my voice, keep it flat, calm, steady: 'There is nothing wrong with me.'

(I have also not yet learned that it's useless and dangerous to defend myself, that I am making it worse.)

THE ARCHER: Stupid Winona gets it wrong. Again.

I do know that this time I cannot back down. My only option, according to articles I find on High-Conflict Communication with Challenging Personalities, is to detach physically and emotionally from any communication: avoid eye contact, act unresponsive, do not show emotion, become as boring as possible and hope this will make the dangerous person lose interest. The advice is to transform yourself into a 'grey rock'. This is hard to do when neither I nor the children can detach physically or emotionally from the consequences of the communication.

Grey-rocking is a version of playing dead. I have yet to master this; I am more like the ptarmigan who mimics a broken wing to distract the predators from her babies: *look at me — easy prey — chase this, maul this, over here!*

I consult an online article in the National Library of Medicine. It is most helpful in explaining further: for small-bodied motherbirds who take sole charge of their young, aggression is not a viable option because the parent poses no risk to the predator. The mother therefore must utilise deceptive strategies to protect her young. This is referred to as 'Nest Defence Behaviour'.

(n.b. The escalation of the deceptive behaviour is dictated by the degree of predation.)

It is possible to make a small yet elegant list of the Ways of Defence:

MOTHERBIRD NEST DEFENCE BEHAVIOUR:
- catching the predator's eye
- false brooding
- the 'rodent run'

(Perhaps tears could be included in the nest defence arsenal.)
Grey rock, grey stone, granite mountain — mountain fountain brighten tighten titan woodsmen groundsmen badmen frighten —

I imagine myself a snow-crowned mountain haloed by Beethoven's Fifth symphony — the opening bars (*short-short-short-long*) making the morse letter V — Churchill's symbol of resistance, and the secret signal sent on 1 June 1944 to France to prepare for an Allied attack. Five days later, the largest amphibious invasion in history hit the beaches of Normandy: Operation OVERLORD, also known as D-Day.

But what ground is being fought for here? We cannot both be mountains. Which one of us, then, the iceberg?

(short-short-short-long)

I do realise that I should be recording the phone conversation; I should be finding a way to show someone what He is saying, that He is lying. I fumble with the phone, but I have no idea how to record anything, and I'm shaking so much it falls from my hand.

As it falls, I hear His roar —

I'M GOING TO FUCK YOUR LIFE!

One of my legs gives way, and I list to one side and come to sit softly on the grass. I turn my face away from the fig tree and vomit quietly into the grass.

liar mire tyre pyre dire briar desire fire

I breathe a moment and then turn and wave to the kids, my smile wide.

'I'm coming up the tree! Wait for me!'

love it shove it move it lose it prove it; twit lit sit mitt kit knit bit

In the branches of the massive tree, we pretend we are orangutans, and this is our home; we hug the different branches and feel them creak and move in the wind.

'Can you believe this is a tree?! It's like a rhinoceros — look at its skin, look how huge its branches are!'

'It's like an elephant!'

'Or our house — a pirate ship!'

We climb higher: elevation as a physical expression of joy — tinged with dark relief — but Joy! We feel safe off the ground, protected by the ancient mother tree. In the distance, the top of a megamall, signposted in red, is just visible over the trees, and they sway, and it all feels so far away. I close my eyes, my cheek on the trunk, and I sway, too.

Winona is not an easy one. It can be made to rhyme, with varying degrees of closeness, with:

aphonia (loss of voice), dysphonia (speech impediment), begonia, mahonia (evergreen shrub), paulownia (Japanese tree), pneumonia, ammonia, bignonia (tropical shrub), boronia (aromatic shrub), claytonia (succulent plant), boltonia (flowering plant), houstonia (flowering plant), Slavonia (region of the defunct Yugoslavia), eudemonia (happiness), catatonia (a form of schizophrenia), anisekonia (visual defect), bronchopneumonia, pleuronemonia.

Winona does not rhyme with sunny or money or honey.

I don't want to read too much into this. It is not a sign, it is not an omen, it is not an onomastic mantle I wish to wear.

I'M ON MY WAY home from the brain scan, my long, anxious fingers worrying the gobs of wax still stuck in my hair, leaning against the door in the backseat of an Uber. It is still early enough for morning traffic, snaking down the hill, an anaconda today, a Titanoboa... There is not enough room for all the cars on the road. The system of calculated stops and starts — winking horizontal moves, inch-by-inch creeps, red lights, headlights, amber lights, green lights missed, horns wild with frustration — is straining, and we are one mis-timed acceleration away from total chaos.

A westerly wind blows in dots and dashes, bringing hot air from the interior — a brickfielder wind, given body by particles of red sand and the ash from the bushfires so that it flows between the stationary cars in grubby currents. Dervishes of reddish air spin in tight twists, clutch leaves, draw them upwards then fling them out as if in disgust. The gusts, threading their way through car bumpers and telephone wires, setting them singing and whistling and screaming, reek of burning. It is unsettling and unhealthy air; it swells the eyes and sits painfully on the upper chest, like grief.

I braid my fingers, grateful not to be behind the wheel.

THE ARCHER: You know ...

They begin speaking slowly, deliberately, slyly drawing back the vowels to telegraph the imminent release of a poisoned arrow:

THE ARCHER: You know, don't you, that you were never expected to survive your divorce?

Now it is as if every breath of air inside the car has been vacuumed up and sent to play outside. The wind pours faster down the hill, a river of dirty cloud setting off car alarms, smearing torn plastic bags onto hedges, and snagging branches, sucking at the coat of the lone pedestrian shielding her face at the lights.

THE NANNY: Face front. Don't move. Sit still. Do not acknowledge the comment, Winona.

The car rolls forward an inch then rocks as a punch of wind hits it from the side. A broken tree branch flies past the windscreen, as thick as a baby's arm, scraping the roof. The driver brakes suddenly with a cry and turns to me, palms raised to the window. I nod, also jump-scared, and widen my eyes in acknowledgement:

Yes! I, too, witnessed that! That happened! We are in this together. We will come out of this together.

My seatbelt is too tight, too high; it pulls at the jugular notch at the base of my throat. I tug to loosen it, but the safety catch won't release, draws down tighter even.

THE ARCHER: I know you heard me ...

Those vowels again. I brace.

THE ARCHER: You know I am right. There's no point pretending this is anything but a situation primed to be apocalyptic for you. He has done well.

I stop further head-conversation by asking the driver to please turn up the volume on the radio. He is happily surprised, happy to oblige. We each hope the distraction will ease our respective tension, even for a moment. (I also hope my passenger rating will reflect this felicitous request: this has also been a consideration.)

The radio, however, cannot resist predicting the apocalypse: almost two hundred consecutive days of fire emergency, and still the winds will not let up. The flames of the fires are being fanned by this dry breath that seems to issue from the mouth of hell itself. Koalas with burnt paws scream, homes are torched, acres of ignited eucalypts are creating fireballs up and down the east coast. A tornado of flames in the south-west lifts a fire truck into the air and smashes it down, killing those inside. Sand has vitrified, and the roads are melting. In one coastal town, people are running to the beach to escape the fires, but they will soon be trapped between the ocean and the flames. The air is barely breathable, and the firefighters are down to their bare bones. The army has been mobilised.

In the cities, haze has smudged all horizons brown. The surf deposits charcoal and charred branches on the tideline, leaving huge black fans of detritus on the white sand. Children are kept indoors, and sports are suspended as great flakes of ash fall from the sky, dark snow.

There are no stable images — everything flickers and explodes and is half-obscured by smoke — and there is no silence: sirens, car alarms, distressed dogs; the velvet tear of gales around concrete corners ... Soda cans are lifted from bins and rip down the street until they bash themselves against a wall. Banshees keen all night.

Everyone is on edge.

Portents loom too big, too close, too fast ... too much cosmic information is sweeping through my brain — vast, fast-connecting constellations of meaning, foreshadowments and harbingers, omens, visions, messages and manifestations threaten to spiral me ...

I slip on my ear defenders instead. They are large and black, and sit around my neck almost all the time, just in case. I have recently discovered noise-cancelling mode, and it can bring respite from overwhelm, so they have become a life-ring of sorts.

The cushions softly cup my ears and immediately there is a sweet feeling of relief, like cool water, or blood flowing into a long-tense muscle. This morning, silence seems like it might be fraught with perils, and so I choose music.

THE POET: Naturally, you must match the drama of the squalls outside — this is an opportunity to heighten all sensation, to swell with emotion, to match the weather ... to raise and carry the day, to transform the ordinary moment into something transcendental!

The Poet is easily agitated in inclement weather. Meanwhile, the vowel archer squats silently in the shadows, watching to see what happens next, biding her time, no doubt. I choose to ignore her and focus on the music.

Only Maria Callas can trump traffic and gales and an unstable internal weather system today; only her voice can supersede: Casta Diva, with Callas as the high priestess offering her prayer to the goddess of the moon — the moment of stillness before the war and every heartstring stripped for plucking, volume high. I put on my thick black sunglasses and pull up the dark hood of my jumper. I create a Comfortable Stable Environment; I disappear.

The traffic swells and recedes, and I am carried.

THE ARCHER: I'll be quiet *if* you tell me I'm wrong.

(It seems the archer does not like being ignored.)

Casta Diva, che inargenti queste sacre antiche piante ...

— the silvering moon, the sacred plants —

THE ARCHER: You mortgaged your future to His fear and gave two hostages to fortune—

Stop.

... punirlo io posso. (Ma punirlo, il cor non sa)

— I can punish him, but my heart —

THE ARCHER: He has been offered multiple opportunities to be merciful in small ways. Each time, He has chosen not to be; each time, He has chosen to exert maximum pressure and to be as cruel as the situation allowed.

(THE POET: This is the measure of a man.)

I take off my sunglasses, because it is unkind to talk without your eyes: 'Thank you,' I say to the driver, pushing back my hood, lowering the headphones around my neck, offering a smile. 'You can drop me here. It's close enough.' (This last part is largely unnecessary, as the car is not moving, but I say it anyway, as if this were a normal day and everyone was fine.)

I slip out of the passenger door and across two lanes of stationary traffic, baggy clothes alternately billowing and clinging in the wild, wild wind; I award the driver five stars and add a small tip.

I am a writer of romantic fiction that can no longer summon up the suspension of my own disbelief in the genre to be credible. My heart cannot lie to my readers, and at the moment it does not see 'romance' as a safe place to dwell. I am hoping this will change as I discover new ways to love. Until then, I have taken on several projects doctoring other people's film scripts. It pays well, and I get to keep my own hours, as most of the production companies are in LA or London anyway. It feels pragmatic and sensible to have deadlines, Zoom meetings, a predictable income ... and it's also a comfort to be dealing with Events and Stories Not My Own (mostly heist films, it turns out). The language and structure of the film scripts bleeds into me when I work; it interrupts my day with breakdowns, and I walk as if I am in a film.

I am:

```
EXT. SUBURBAN STREET — DAY

The TREES bend in a gale, stark against
the white sky. WINONA, thin, swamped by a
hoodie, moves furtively for no reason …

Shadows cast on the pavement by the three-
and four-storey tenements make dark, fat-
knuckled fists.
```

A man in a courier's hi-visibility vest and holding a parcel makes as if to approach — perhaps for directions? — and thinks the better of it. My appearance is discouraging. Thin in the way that suggests something has happened to me to melt away flesh — stripped me down — and swamped by oversized clothes; headphones holstered. He looks down at his phone as if this had been his intention all along.

I am carried past him.

Fear hums as a noisy constant in my head, generalised, unfocussed, kept contained only by Tasks and Matters that must be attended to with careful attention. When I stand still, the roaring grows so loud I think I might be driven mad by it.

THE ARCHER: You are already mad.

THE NANNY: Definitions belong to the definers, not the defined.

THE ARCHER: Toni Morrison said that. She was not talking about madness.

(Here The Child chimes in, never wanting to be left out of the conversation.)

THE CHILD: No. No, she wasn't!

THE NANNY: Surely you have proof now that you are not mad.

'Proof' feels too definite a word for what just happened at the hospital.

THE NANNY: A brain scan can be used —

Walk on.

It is too windy for the birds today, surely. Where do they go in the wild weather? It's one of those questions asked by small children that never really get answered to any satisfaction and remain like that for the rest of your life — a patch of fog and suspension in a universe of concrete knowledge. I like to think of them nestling together in some tree hollow, riding out the weather and singing softly to drown out the wind. Are they frightened by the smoke? Fire for birds must have no paradoxically pleasant connotations: the campfire, a haven on a snowy night. Fire is pure alarm.

Perhaps a deep well of species memory tells them where is safe.

Three streets back from the beach, the sand is banking in the gutters, blown across by the wind. Nothing is where it should be: the sand is not on the beach, the bird is not in the nest, the children are not —

The noises the wind makes are loud!
moving through leaves and long grass
rolling a plastic bottle down the street
knocking over a sandwich board
slamming a door

setting off a car alarm

tugging at awnings like errant jibs, the thwacking sound of ropes

the waves roaring

the whistle of air through fine sand whipping small tornadoes that sting your legs if you walk near the beach

careening around the sharp corners of my house, the wind seems to buzz and vibrate the air with a sound more felt than heard, more like a gargantuan mosquito than breath of nature, disconcerting, unsettling

the birds cannot fly and the windchimes have lost their mind

such is the orchestra today

(headphones)

we have no relief; we seek release.

I'M STILL WALKING HOME when I spot Bruce — my non-human neighbour — on the street opposite, with his long, long legs taking their sweet old time. He is almost as tall as a Shetland pony, lean, with a salt-and-pepper pelt and the most extraordinary orange eyes. He is wisely keeping the wind behind him. Our eyes meet in mutual pleasure; he doesn't find me odd, or at least, if he does, he hides it well ... Although he would tell you that animals don't lie. It's one of the reasons humans feel drawn to them. The uncomplicated emotional nature of our relationship is a deep solace and joy for me.

He lopes towards me, crossing the road on a diagonal as dogs are wont to do, and I hold up my palms in welcome and affection.

'Are you as overwhelmed as I am today, Bruce? Your nose must be picking up so much information with this violent wind ...'

I feel exhausted now and sit down on the gutter, my back to the wind. Bruce sits beside me. We look up at the white sky. The light is so strange, greyish and milky with odd glitters — dust? ash? sand? gold? — that for a moment I wonder if I haven't passed through a veil into a dimension similar but also quite different to my own ... The thought pleases me immensely. I place a hand gently on the small of Bruce's back. His fur is rough and reassuring.

BRUCE: How is the state of your heart, in this breath?

This is how he greets me every time, and every time I pause

and think that *this* is a proper question and that this is what we should be asking each other every day.

'Bruce, today I was at the hospital testing for the source of my seizures, and I was remembering my baby, the holding ...'

He takes a moment to sniff the air before replying: It is always about the holding — of heartspace and bodies and all the fallen pieces of what was once and now cannot be — is that what is hurting you?

'I miss my children. I am scared.'

BRUCE: You might think of them as always with you. The transcendence of consciousness within spacetime begins with the experience of dual unity: you are Winona, and you are also your children. You have your heart, and you hold their hearts.

'I do have a Transcendence Project, yes, and it has this very idea at its core. It began as a way to find the deeper meaning of my physical situation — to unite the mundanity of domestic life with the elevated and heavenly experience of the cosmos. It is a project that would harness the tension inherent between the two — that would see the dairy aisle of the supermarket vibrate alongside the contemplation of infinite galaxies and create a third state of being, of harmonic dualism. This project would require that we speak to each other's souls, and smile at screaming toddlers, and very slow drivers, and people shouting into their phones, and we would understand that there is the potential of cosmic glory in every moment if we shift our lens.'

BRUCE: And today?

'Today the structures of the mundane world feel too firm, and I am struggling to move beyond them. I have become numbers and letters and test results, and I risk reduction to the point of being lost altogether.'

BRUCE: You might require a radical paradigm shift, the evolution of your Transcendence Project into something even greater ... What does your soulseed tell you?

'To vanish, to elude, to transform into something wholly ungraspable; to transcend linear time and embrace a fluidity and a porousness that is completely at odds with the protective structure the human world has created to keep us "safe".'

When safe places are not; when safe people are not —

'Inside I feel circles within circles — catching the light and resting lightly on each other, expanding me from within, nested infinities pushing out and obliterating the boxes of both linear time and one-dimensionality.'

BRUCE: The forces of separation are contrary to the universe's unbroken wholeness. Striving for separateness goes against the universe's longing for mutual flourishing. Perhaps this is the source of the discomfort you feel.

'Perhaps that is it — the lawyers and divorces and doctors and tests; the spreadsheets and appointments and deadlines and material screams of "MINE!" are forces of division and separation.'

BRUCE: You seek unity.

'I seek unity and mutual flourishing.'

BRUCE: If you cannot at least imagine you are free, you are living a life that is all wrong for you. What small acts can you undertake to further the cause of freedom?

'I liberate plants — I rescue them. (Sometimes I take them.)'

The pause here is long, and my head fills with the sounds of rustling leaves that may be coming from the tree near me, or from Bruce, or from an as-yet undefined source ...

THE PLANTS: Perhaps we in turn take you —

BRUCE: Perhaps they in turn take you.
THE PLANTS: We liberate you —
(I'm surer now that the rustling whispered this.)
THE PLANTS: Liberate yourself from vexed hierarchies
Consider the more-than-human world

Soften the underpinnings of modern thought that would have you trapped, Winona.

I close my eyes and allow the world to pass through me. This, too, is a form of transcendence — being alive to Other Perceivers, receptive to their energetic incursions, malleable, visible in other ways ...

Bruce stands and gives himself a shake; I stand also.

BRUCE: Have you considered that your temporal lobe seizures are connected to your fraught relationship with time?

'No, I ...'

And I drift ...

BRUCE: In moments of acute temporal crises, consider the contemplation of glaciology: deep time is the total collapse of the present.

He gives his tail a little wag — a half-wag — and turns to go.

BRUCE: Walk on.

And I walk on.

THERE IS A PHOTOGRAPH on the fridge that I should probably not have stuck there. It's an image of the boys and my parents, a friend of theirs from Zimbabwe on the left. My mother is smiling and has her arm around my elder son, who grins happily. He is in the photograph, too, although I have managed to hide most of Him under a menu of Vietnamese food options for take-away. I am holding my youngest boy in my arms — he might have been three. My hair is brushed back into a smooth ponytail I no longer recognise; my shoulders hunch forward, hanging over my heart, and my dress has a floral print — bright, loud, happy, too big. I can tell I am exhausted, despite the cheerful colours; I can see that despite my masquerade, my fatigue has run beyond the need for sleep and become a chronic soul-condition.

THE NANNY: Here you have revealed yourself in the very moment you thought you were hiding!

(It was a Passive Deception Strategy.)

A cursory glance could still yield the intended information: 'Happy family, happy housewifemotherperson' but my eyes, sliding to gaze out of frame, my face partially hidden behind my son's dear head, the draping, drooping dress, makes it clear that I am losing the desire to please anyone, and mostly, the desire to please myself.

THE ARCHER: Ladies and Gentlemen —

The snide and mocking voice of the ringmaster arrives now in full throat, pointing to the photograph with their cane.

THE ARCHER: Here we have a classic case of Falling Baseline Syndrome!

THE CHILD: That's like the Frog in the Pot!

A small voice that the assembled crowd ignores, excited by the ringmaster's verbal flourishes, by the promise of cruelty.

THE ARCHER: Where the subject, WINONA, has allowed herself to completely forget what used to be her normal way of being! What a pathetic creature, ladies and gentlemen.

All faces in photographs have an innate deficiency. It's why we adopt poses. My stance in the photograph told a story I didn't yet have words for. These had been the start of the Grey Days, and for an instant I re-feel their emotional charge. I am paralysed and sick and hot, all at once. My chest compresses under some invisible weight. The trembling re-begins ...

I open the fridge door — motion the antidote, purpose the Ultimate Distraction — and reach for the milk. I remind myself to remember to find another photo to tether my children to their family, their happy memories. The trembling has spread from my fingers to my hands to my arms. There is no milk in the fridge. My molars taste of metal.

THE NANNY: You were desperate to find a way to believe in the future again.

I was. So desperate I had to break everything.

THE POET: Freedom was impossible any other way. It was you who was being pushed out of the family photograph. All the words were in the language of diminution, designed to close the mind, to reduce to nothingness. You moved so far over to make more room for Him that you fell out of your own life. It was nothing short of attempted murder.

I think you exaggerate.

THE POET: I think there are many ways to kill a person.

Fridge door suctioning shut; the photograph again.

THE NANNY: You did not rip Him out of the picture though, even though he is conveniently — temptingly, even — positioned at the outer edge of the group.

I did not.

I have thought about it, though. It's a gesture that would make sense to an onlooker, to an audience if I were playing myself in a film. But it would not carry the charge of authenticity. I cannot summon the passion of emotion required for this to be an organic tearing. I remain numb. The photograph remains intact.

And tearing it would send the wrong message to the children. I don't want to deprive the children of their past just because of my unhappy memories! And so, the photo stays, curling the lips of its corners.

THE POET: What of your memories? You wish to unknow what you know. You are actively trying to forget. How can you reconcile this paradox of Motivated Forgetting?

My desire is to grow past, over, and around; my intention is to escape like ivy and to regain my store of Tomorrows.

(All the things we cannot see are most alive for me.)

THE NANNY: This is your problem. His greatest strength lies in His lack of imagination. He cannot see through your eyes, He cannot feel with your nerves. You will always come off worse with a man like this.

He nicknamed the violence and called it love —

THE ARCHER: That is a well-trodden path. It is a cliché. There is no imagination in that.

I nod and wipe the kitchen bench, already clean.

The house is too tidy, the oppression of an order that craves disturbance and yet remains stubbornly As Is. The hum of an empty day can grow to deafen you if you don't stay focussed. I fill the water levels in the jars of my rescue plants, Tending Mothercare suddenly flowing out of me. With nowhere to go, no receptacle, that sort of love becomes tears, becomes deposits into a well of loneliness.

The poinsettia. I mist her with water, her velvety leaves tender between my fingers.

Love must be expressed and received and you, orphan plantlings, shall be the recipients. I beam at you.

I will see the boys for a picnic this evening. I have shopped for their favourite foods at the supermarket. I shop less frequently now that I am alone so much. Yesterday, as I drifted in through the double doors of Woolworths, I realised I almost missed it; there had occurred a shift in my lens. It struck me that the supermarket exists as an extension of the domestic space. It exists to help feed a family, friends. With no clocks, confined and windowless, the activities that take place within it are invisible, trivial, another of the tasks often considered 'women's work' and devalued accordingly.

It is also a safe place: a public, female space where it is neither strange nor dangerous to be alone, where the tasks required are simple and achievable. It is an anticipatory space: it telegraphs hope for the future, a future that may contain oranges, a soup, bowls of pasta, perhaps a cake to be baked ... Great Literature contains few — if any — supermarkets; they are not the arena of battles and kings and elephants. But those over-lit linoleum aisles are sometimes the site of small and important victories: the decision to choose life, to affirm, to nurture, to persist in loving; to care, to consider, to spend for others, to Keep Going Despite It All.

When the Russian journalist Anna Politkovskaya was assassinated in the foyer of her Moscow apartment — five bullets at point-blank range, one to the head — she was holding a bag of groceries. Outspoken about the evils of Putin's regime and his war in Chechnya, she defied death threats, rape threats, and survived a mock execution to keep on speaking out. Her bag of shopping contained supplies for dinner and also hope for the future. It was a symbol of her determination to keep on living. The last photograph of her is from the CCTV camera of a supermarket, one hour and thirty-nine minutes before her death. She is entering the supermarket, smiling — a quick shop for dinner things for her and her son, Ilya. The image declares her bravery, her humanity; she has no intention of being murdered that evening, and she refuses to live as if she might be. The photograph speaks more truth about her than all the sham trials of her would-be assassins.

The pleasures and terrors of domestic comfort.

Things in my space have been prepared with similar simple hopes for the future: a fridge stocked with small favourites — watermelon juice, little yoghurts, strawberries, olives ...

Don't forget to buy milk for breakfast —

There is a limit to what is possible when using Motivated Forgetting. It is a permeable undertaking with no promises of certainty or success.

THE NANNY: And then they began to run away.

I think of it rather as running towards: they were running towards their mother.

THE ARCHER: That is not how the lawyers and courts saw it.

No. In their looking-glass world, the running was proof I was a bad mother and that the children needed to spend more time with their father.

THE ARCHER: You failed them.

I failed them.

I look around the living room. There is the pillow fort that I have not dismantled, still standing behind the sofa. Weeks ago, now. I force myself to take in the full, sucking power of the absence it evokes. Crashed and dearly dented pillows the evidence of what was fought for there, the ground ceded, the attacks and battle-cries ...

I remember to put one foot in front of the other in moments like these and not to look up until the feeling recedes.

Because Life remains suspended in the gaps between seeing the children. I am on pause, moving without moving, treading air over an abyss I cannot glance down to acknowledge lest I fall.

They say there is a crater in Africa that has no bottom. If you fall, you fall forever. I wonder how long it would take to lose the fear of falling if you were falling forever. I imagine it, a dawn hike, a slippery, rocky scree, then falling ...

At first the rushing wind awakes the terror, your guts heave up, caught in your throat, limbs in windmills you spin — face up, face down — waiting for the crash that will never come, the Great Correction ... How long would it take to lose the fear of falling if you were falling forever? To accept the exception you have been granted from the consequences of gravity? Would you ever? Would you ever — or does everything, given time, become normal? A forever-falling baseline. Does every unacceptable thing become the thing we now accept as the only possible outcome? The focus narrows ... worlds shrink to marbles, horizons to tentative marks made in pencil — hesitant sketches — raging bushfires dim to sparks that extinguish themselves and return to the dark ...

THE NANNY: Gathering wool is only helpful if you are knitting. Focus. Briskly now.

The important thing is to engage all energies, to drag All and Sundry into the moment, to create a perpetual present. This is an important exercise that extends its usefulness into all aspects of life, not just the time shared with children. It is a crucial way of getting through the day, every day. It is grounding, a sea anchor in the swell, a stone in high wind, a cave that offers just enough shelter to make the time survivable.

The children are still in a state of trauma that makes forgetting more important than remembering. Memory is not a safe place yet. I haven't laid the stepping stones.

THE ARCHER: The photos are not helping —

The photos are a minefield. (I take a lot of new photographs. I am trying my heart out to make things okay.)

Photos help make stories out of our past moments so we can remember them. It's not always possible to do this from the inside out. It is also not always possible to rewrite the stories we don't want to tell anymore. That might require a miracle of sorts.

THE NANNY: Well, there are no photographs of miracles. You said so yourself.

(There might be times when I can be wrong.)

THE NANNY: I will bear that in mind, your occasional unreliability, when placing my trust in you.

You and the World.

I have been standing here too long. A bumblebee is caught between the window and the sun. I will catch it with a glass and a piece of paper and release it outside. I wonder how much it will understand of the glass and the paper I slide beneath it, the movement through space, the release.

I know that the bumblebee sees the heart of a sunflower as ultraviolet, while human perceivers read the seeds as black.

There is surely a portal in this to some greater way of being, of thinking, some door — some thousand doors even — that can be opened into a different space entirely, that can help us to be free, help us move past ourselves.

A human can perceive only the smallest range of colour waves — between violet and red. Our eyes cannot register ultraviolet light, radio rays, cosmic rays. If we were bumblebees or giant squid, bananas might be blue. Birds have a protein in their eyes that lets them see the earth's magnetic fields — their magnetoreception allows them to navigate their migrations, to orientate themselves with the earth below, to find their way.

THE CHILD: Chickens see the sun's rays as ultraviolet! They notice it beginning to rise an hour before we do. And so, the rooster, servant of the sun, crows and wakes the humans!

Yes! You see?! And bananas are blue under ultraviolet light! Everything is equally evolved! Everything is conscious! This is the way freedom lies —

THE ARCHER: You are beginning to sound as mad as they say you are.

The hard edges of the world, strictures, structures, limitations, will not yield and yet, our vision remains mutable despite them. We can choose what we pay attention to. It is our response that validates a structure!

I place the glass over the bee on the window and carefully slide a sheet of paper between the glass and the bee, so I don't touch its delicate bee-ness with huge human fingers.

Can you see how that can be a form of resistance?! Antagonism is the reductive force. It wants to shape How You See. It wants to hijack your frames of reference, limit your options. It will shout at you and make you too scared to think and you won't be able to escape — adrenaline swarm. Refuse the lens! Set your own parameters for engagement.

I slide the window open and release the bee.

Step into other Umwelten and expand ...

Become the plant ...

... go through the veil ...

... step out of the zombie dance.

I move my hands like a murmuration of swallows now, expressing feelings beyond words that head straight for the heart to lodge there and dislodge tears. (Not only sadness now.)

I am a lake perpetually about to spill.

THE NANNY: Focus on facts. You cannot cripple yourself by collapsing into Feeling. There are practicalities that must be attended to. Your car has a flat tyre.

That's why I walk.

And now the silence within and without is deafening.

THE ARCHER: No, it's not.

Chastened, I reach for the phone to find the name of the tyre place.

Resist. Refuse. Roam. Do not accept.

'Hello?'

The tyre man sounds nice when he answers the phone: kind, helpful, uncle-y. A tear escapes my eye.

'I can drive it in. It's just losing air. Maybe a nail ... Oh wonderful. Okay. Thank you.'

A very small shiver of satisfaction courses through me at

having exchanged information and made a pragmatic plan.

The car will be fixed and ready for the boys after school!

(But I will not bring the car in today. I am not allowed to drive. My seizures have temporarily disqualified me. The comfort is in knowing I could make the call. In a world just like this one, only different, I take the car to be repaired and go to collect the boys, like I do every day, and everything is normal and the same outside as it is inside.)

The boys would come this afternoon if permission was granted. Their father was not speaking directly to me; He was speaking through a lawyer with a reputation for extreme aggression. She said He would go to the court and have me declared mad, unfit, a danger to the children, and they would be taken away from me unless I agreed to what He wanted.

<u>PHRASES THAT ARE TOO DANGEROUS TO SPEAK ALOUD:</u>

by Winona Dalloway

- ~~wards of the court~~
- ~~emergency court order~~
- ~~supervised access~~
- ~~suing for full custody~~

These must be immediately crossed off the list; they are the Damoclean Daggers that He has strung above me like so many evil fairy lights.

The seizures had happened the day after the email came from his lawyer —

From The Offices of Frances Hodgson & Burnett LLP
Dear Mrs Dalloway,

> This is to inform you —
> Please find attached —
> The affidavit below —
> Response required within —

While I was in hospital the boys had had to go to their father, and now He would not let them come back.

I could see them on His terms or not at all.

Battles can be fought in courts, more lawyers hired, more experts subpoenaed ... I have been down this road before. I showed the lawyers the hospital reports, written by nurses, counsellors, paediatricians, but it felt like no one was listening, that I was shouting from behind bulletproof glass, screaming with my kids distraught beside me. It did no good. Nothing made any difference. The blame and onus of proof kept falling onto me and onto the children. And so deep down I have no faith in a system, in systems, that up until now have only done more harm than good.

Why should this outcome be any different? Reports, boxes, depositions, judges — I know how the rectilinear world deals with circles, and this is not a gamble I am prepared to even risk losing, not even 0.05%. I've seen the charm offensives in action. I know how He would play it — I can hear His voice reasoning amiably, sensibly, man-to-man, or flattering a woman with His undivided attention; I can see the perfect cut of His suit, and I know who will come off worst. Every room I have been in with Him has delivered the same outcome.

'The mother is resisting her diagnosis.'

The email from the lawyers had also informed me that Professor Beale-Brown from the MYND institute (silver beard;

purple carpet) has recently written a report at His request. My appointment with him had been during the darker of the Days Before, when my fading, my deep melancholy, my refusal to participate in the social dance around me had been identified as a Medical Problem That Could — indeed *Must!* — Be Solved.

(Here my mind makes a quick and inevitable list — the tethering power of the lists! Where would I be without them and did making so many lists make me mad?)

THE NANNY: *Focus*, Winona.

<u>MEDICAL PROBLEMS THAT CAN BE SOLVED</u>

By Winona Dalloway

- a fractured wrist or foot; other skeleton-related damage
- short- or long-sightedness (no we can't put innervision on the list because although it can be a problem if it begins to dominate the patient there is no medical solution yet)
- a rash (usually, unless it's something difficult like Lyme disease)
- a sore throat and/ or tonsilitis and most of the 'itises'

The list for those problems that cannot be solved is longer and more obscure, but Professor Beale-Brown of the MYND institute does not see it that way. For him, everything has a scientific solution, and every problem is a medical one that harnesses the Godpower of doctors and their drugs to work miracles on the physiognomy, which, according to him, includes the mind. (No mention is made of the soul at that appointment, but that is for another time ...) There are no mysteries for Professor

Beale-Brown that he cannot unravel with this paradigm.

THE POET: Winona, you are a prisoner of a false paradigm.

THE ARCHER: Hardly the first time ...

mad, bad, sad, lad, cad, dad, olympiad; dryad, nyad, Hyderabad, Gallahad —

THE NANNY: FOCUS, WINONA.

After a questionnaire that asks so many questions except the single right one, Professor Beale-Brown declares that I am quite likely bipolar and most certainly require medication. (As Professor Beale-Brown's institute is dedicated to the study of mood disorders with a focus on bipolar, this is not a surprising outcome. I can hear my father's words — 'never ask a barber', etc.)

I imagine the professor's satisfaction as he signs at the bottom of the page — remember his self-conscious tweed jacket, his framed diplomas, framed photographs of prominent people shaking his hand at galas ... On that afternoon, my questions about his famous Questionnaire were not appreciated; it seems they now factor in his new report as evidence that I was 'uncooperative'.

THE CHILD: What was the right question? The one he didn't ask?

Really?

THE CHILD: Yes.

I breathe deeply. Thoughts of the Past threaten to collapse my shaky timeline.

Hold taut the line between Then and Now, ratchet it steady.

I suspend all else and stretch my wingtips, fingers out, close my eyes, and become Philippe Petit, the high-wire artist, walking the forty metres between the twin towers of New York with no net, suspended 412 metres above the city.

Is there anything going on in your life right now that might account for your low mood and/or mood fluctuations?

This simple question had remained unasked. I remember the sap rising in my ears, the blood, as I reached the end of the questionnaire and realised that nothing True would be revealed in these rooms, that everything important would be left unsaid, and that a myth based on false assumptions would be spun and it Would Not End Well for me.

I remember that outside, a swarm of cicadas was screeching — had they been there all along? — jet engines in constant take-off, revving, deafening. They became the sound of the summer heat itself, radiating through the professor's tinted window.

Cicadas, by the way, are the loudest insect on the planet, up to 120 decibels, another fact my children know. They live underground for seven years, burrowed in the earth, sucking on the sap of tree roots, then burst their way out. They have a week, maybe two, to shed their exoskeletons: they must inhabit this crisis when emergence from what came before must be total and abrupt. This is the *instar*, the stage between two successive moults, when the early moments of change mimic deterioration and where the cicada is most vulnerable. No wonder they scream. I had let the sound roll through me like surf or thunder.

What you resist only grows stronger.
No wonder they are screaming.

No doubt it pleases Professor Beale-Brown that, as a respectable hammer of the community, he can be brought to bear on errant nails, on a loose screw who refuses to recognise that she is a screw and must be twisted firmly, tightly, into the wall.

That sort of language will not help you in court.

THE ARCHER: Precisely.

THE NANNY: And so, we are at a juncture where —

Stop. Let me say it. Your vocabulary makes it all sound too permanent. Nothing is set in stone. No courts are involved yet, no police are coming for me —

THE ARCHER: This time —

No police are coming for me. I will see the boys this evening.

THE ARCHER: You hope.

(There will be a bodyguard with them.)

THE ARCHER: Could you say that again, please? Louder, so we can hear you in the back.

There will be a bodyguard with them.

Fortunately, the bee has been let outside or its humming right now would deafen me. Instead, a distant concrete saw grinds fiercely into cement. Into my head.

A court war would destroy me, already on my bare bones, and it would rip the children to shreds.

THE NANNY: He knows that. He is gambling on you not fighting.

Even an infinitesimal risk of loss is unacceptable in this equation. I cannot take that decision for the kids. Their childhood cannot be dominated by a horrible war. It is all they will remember.

THE CHILD: You must make other memories for them, whatever the cost to you. You must make sure they have a childhood.

I have tried to go limp in my heartache ... become immovable by my sheer softness. (You cannot break water.)

THE POET: You could think of it as an act of civil disobedience —

THE NANNY: Defence is the first act of war —

THE ARCHER: And now He is making you pay for a bodyguard to keep the children safe from you.

It is temporary ...

THE ARCHER: You must pay for a bodyguard to be able to see your children.

(Yes.)

THE POET: The ironies are not lost on —

In this world where that is allowed to happen, anything can, and I can't risk it.

THE NANNY: It will drive you mad.

THE ARCHER: That's the point.

THE POET: To climb out of the pit, you must stop digging and begin to build a ladder.

THE NANNY: Unhelpful. This crater has no bottom. What use a ladder? Were you not listening earlier?

THE POET: Then you will fall out the other side.

I pause. This image pleases me: falling out — falling up — on the other side of the world. I pop, in my mind, like a joyful gopher from a hole in the earth.

THE POET: You cannot go back, you cannot stop and fight, you must go through.

Then that is what I shall do. I shall absorb longing and heartbreak and humiliation and fear so that I might fall up the other side. I will focus on the joys and expand; I will swell like an ocean into which the rivers of silt pour.

(I shall transcend.)

I let a tear become as heavy as it can and watch it drop in

fullness onto my To-Do List. It blurs the word 'call'. (I can cross that item off now. More satisfaction, more proof of viability as a human.)

- ~~Call tyre man~~
- buy milk

THE ARCHER: Your ocean appears to have burst its banks.
Okay. You need to leave me alone now. You have said your piece.

That tear now disappearing into the paper will be a Tear of Relief tinged with Desperation, nudging the border with Elation. Mixed feelings. I had seen, years ago, a series of photographs by Rose-Lynn Fisher, taken with a Zeiss lens and a microscope, of the crystalline structure of tears. Trapped between slides of glass, the photographs had revealed each tear to be made up of unique crystals, like snowflakes or quartz deposits — an emotional topography that blew my mind and yet made perfect sense. The photographs had completely enchanted me and haunt me yet.

There had been much crying in my homeworld at the time of my discovery. It seemed as if the lakes of emotion that the children and I carried within us were bottomless. Only exhaustion stemmed the flow … or a kind of numbness that froze the trickle from my eyes, an imposed forgetfulness, a stunned distraction, head heavy, red eyelids full of sand. Constantly heavy, all day. The relief that was supposed to come from tears never came. They pooled somewhere inside, lapping at my edges, ever-present but invisible, the physical manifestation of a total emotional overwhelm.

Tears have taken the space vacated by words, their inadequacy keenly felt here — no words, not enough words, not the right words, no space left for Words.

THE POET: Camus urges: Live to the point of tears.

I am living past the point of tears.

(There is a frozen lake of tears at my core and before you point out the melodrama of this image, I borrowed it from Dante's ninth circle of hell — in *la Divina Commedia* — from his lake Cocytus, made from the tears shed by Lucifer and kept frozen by the wind created as he flaps his satanic wings. The ninth circle of Dante's Inferno houses The Treacherous — those who have betrayed special bonds of love and trust. A lake of tears is a proscribed trope then, but no less real for that. It is perhaps, in fact, realer.)

Fisher's photographs show the structure of tears like aerial maps of previously undiscovered landscapes — seascapes, cities, cells, snow. Each tear is as unique as a snowflake, as uniquely beautiful. The true miracle is that the salty residue formed by the tears takes on wildly different shapes according to the kind of tear that is shed; their topography depends on why we are crying.

THE NANNY: The topography of our tears depends on why we are crying.

THE POET: Perhaps then there *are* photographs of miracles. Yet another chance for Awe and Wonder; one more chance for a heart to skip a beat.

I cry with the onion, the sand in my eye, the wind too sharp, too cold. These are tears of physical irritation, basal tears. They are structurally different from tears shed from exhaustion — or from anger, from the loss of a beloved friend, from laughter, rapture. Delicate structures reach out from inside us to silently perform, in the physical, our emotional states.

Emotion can only exist perfectly in the absence of words. And so, tears take over, run like rivers over cheeks, straight from the source of it all. They build and swell, they pour, trickle, well. There is an arc to their falling and flowing, like a concerto: a progression, most often, to release.

THE CHILD: Crying is what you do when you can't talk.

THE NANNY: It's not safe for a woman to talk, but it is usually safe for a woman to cry.

THE POET: Well, tears remain indistinct, can more easily be misattributed to your advantage. This is a useful thing when safe places are not —

THE ARCHER: (When safe people are not —)

THE POET: Remember the ptarmigan — hold your broken wing aloft.

(Tears would most definitely be in the nest defence arsenal.)

Look closely at Fisher's photographs: fractals are at work. Tear-crystals mimic jagged cliffs, others dry creek beds or snowflakes, coral formation, algae, frozen lakes. All sense of scale and perspective falls away — we are inside something enormous and unknowable, an undiscovered terrain that is microscopic and yet cosmic in its scope.

Deep time on display, deep time interacting with human time. This nexus holds all the potential for poetry.

The Museum of Lace and Fashion in Calais collaborated with Fisher to design lace based on her tear-crystal images. Imagine walking the streets of Lisbon or Paris or Naples wearing a dress made of Tears of Longing, or perhaps of Elation? Perhaps your body would response on a cellular level to the call of geometry, to the simultaneous crumpling of human time, and the elevation and expansion of the moment itself.

I spin.

A list of some of Fisher's gentle titles for her photographs:
- 'tears for those who yearn for liberation'
- 'tears of elation at a liminal moment'
- 'ending and beginning'
- 'redemption'

<u>POTENTIAL TITLES FOR MY TEARS</u>
by Winona Dalloway
- Tears of Overwhelm
- What Couldn't Be Fixed
- The Pull Between Attachment and Release
- Compassion for You
- Take-off
- Momentum, Redirected
- Tears of Change and Terror

Yesterday I saw a tiny boy in the supermarket screaming in fury at his mother, eyes streaming. I imagine *his* tear crystals. When you start to notice crying, it's everywhere: elderly couples hold hands and tear-up in television advertisements; the woman in the mall on facetime to Brazil — home is so far away! A teenager hides red-faced behind a curtain of hair at the back of the bus ...

Mundane, miraculous tears: we are the totality, and we are nothing.

Like Jean Genet's flowers and flags, tears do much of the talking for us.

I think for a moment about Bruce and whether we have talked

about crying, about whether non-humans cry for emotional reasons. His discretion makes it unlikely he would have brought up the subject himself, even if he had seen me weeping. They say it's anthropomorphic and disrespectful to attribute human emotions to non-humans; I think one might also make the counter-argument and say it is reductive and disrespectful to imagine them incapable of our emotions. Bruce is subtle and sensitive, and has more consideration for my feelings than any of my humans.

My eyes flick left to a row of empty glass jars neatly stacked. I have trouble throwing them away — they might one day be useful — and now they have taken up three shelves in my kitchen. They gleam, clean and expectant, lids lightly resting on top.

I imagine the lakes I would have to cry to fill all those jars ...

> You have stored my tears in your bottle and counted each of them. (David to God in the *Old Testament*)

It would be awkward to cry into a bottle, very self-conscious. Like the ripping of the photograph, it feels like the gesture — although undoubtedly poetic — would struggle to feel authentic, to resonate with the true chord of my griefs. In Victorian times, when people in mourning stored their tears in bottles, the period of mourning was over when all the tears had evaporated. Lovers wrenched apart — the soldiers and sailors and mercenaries of the world — kept tear bottles, too. The thought had enchanted me once — enchants me still, although I have trouble holding onto thoughts of Love. They slip through my mind, either jangling in an artificial technicolour or floating belly up like dead fish.

Because there is no tragic register for divorce; no grieving widow to comfort, no casseroles to bake, no wake, no one to pop over and make tea, no tear bottles to fill, no lace handkerchiefs to flourish with gallantry; no violets, no mantillas, no requiems, no coffin, no cake. There can be no beautiful photographs in heavy frames placed carefully by the bed. Divorce is a singularly unromantic series of events that sets people's teeth on edge and compels them to avert their eyes and leave the room as quickly as they can. Like madness, it is a kind of contagion, to be avoided at all costs.

The shame bears down on me still.

> It's such a secret place, the land of tears. (Antoine de Saint-Exupéry, *The Little Prince*)

I wrote the sentence on my wall one evening. Underneath it, on another evening, I wrote:

> Somewhere, something incredible is waiting to be known. (Carl Sagan)

Because this is a beginning and not an end.

I begin rearranging the jars in order of height. It is a useless task.

I will become the collector of my own vale of tears. I will build a cathedral, cry a forest, weep a whole avalanche of snowflakes. There will be an entirely new topography within which to live a life and it will be mine.

THE NANNY: It might be good not to refer to this new topography when talking to the Knowing People. They like to name things, and this new direction might be given an unhelpful name.

Such as?

THE NANNY: I don't need to say it out loud. You know how dangerous those categories are for you. It's better if we leave that unsaid.

I keep my hands busy with more Doing, wiping a little cobweb from a rescued money tree, tipping the rest of my water into the basil plant.

A million different acts of resistance carried out in the home, movements to affirm life, to express love — mainly though a refusal to accept, a refusal to be driven mad or to die.

There was a list, but it was not safe to write it down:

<u>PEOPLE WHO DO NOT LISTEN</u>
By Winona Dalloway
- Doctors

I had added my GP to this list when my son and I had shyly asked for help in his surgery, when my son was five and I was desperate. I had allowed my son to speak, small and eloquent, trusting, about Troubling Times at Home. I, too, had spoken what I had felt to be unspeakable, but I had known this doctor for a long time. He could certainly help us.

His response had been both confusing and staggering — 'Everyone has one shit parent' — and then he had smiled. I remember he'd seemed inordinately pleased with his answer. What I can't remember is if I replied. I don't think I had been able to find the words.

As often as I turn that moment over, I cannot find a slot of the right shape in my mind to let it through. It remains there, a shining, spinning ten-cent piece, unaccepted, and yet devastating in its indifference, in its miscalculation.

Tears of Isolation and Gnawing Dread, Tinged with Shame.

The list has grown, of people who will not understand, who are reluctant to listen, who charge by the hour when they do, whose misinterpretations carry more weight than those of the other people because of their profession:

- Lawyers
- Judges
- Psychiatrists
- Child psychologists
- The police

(It is a small but powerful list; I hope it won't swell)
When safe places are not.
When safe people are not.

> Everywhere on earth, with every day that dawns, a woman stands surrounded by men ready to *throw stones at her*. (Annie Ernaux (her italics), *A Girl's Story*.)

I REMEMBER I HAD been turning to page sixty-five in a state of relaxed receptivity when I read that, and it was as if cymbals had crashed in my ears, as if an orange had been dropped into a sock and swung, hitting me in the solar plexus. I could not put the book down; nor could I read on. I was frozen in the truth of it. The roaring was so loud, the current so strong that if I moved in the slightest, my fingerhold would slip, and I would be washed away forever. After a moment, I slowly reached for my pen, without taking my eyes off the page, and underlined the sentence. Only then could time resume.

And now to glide towards the glass doors at the front of the house. A small forest of rescue plants — monsteras, more money trees, dwarf palms, two poinsettias growing in a single pot; an agave, the top half of a 'chihuahua' plant covered in flecks of white house paint, half a small frangipani tree, too traumatised still to flower — check the water levels, draw the linen curtain all the way across to cut the fierce heat.

My foundlings.

There is constant construction in my neighbourhood, and the plants bear the brunt of builders' damage: boots, trucks, house paint, concrete mix, steel beams the size of houses. And the wind has made for many new additions; the succulents don't bend like the palms, they snap, then lie as broken limbs on the pavement. I bring them home. Most of these plants are very hardy and they thrive in large jars of water, growing root systems that filter the water in the jars, so they never have to be cleaned.

We are in a reciprocal relationship of mutual repair.

On hot days, I carry a small spray bottle for misting.

My hand on the spray bottle, the mist; my hand the mist, my eyes the water jars.

THE POET: Only the thinnest membrane holds you. It threatens to split and to dissolve, and you will lose your integrity.

THE NANNY: Take the elastic bands — right there on the shelf — and place them around your upper arms.

I obey the instructions. I move with economy, tentatively. I slip the rubber bands — one each — onto my upper arms. They grip the skin unpleasantly, tug the fine hairs and then bite and hold. I snap each one in turn, and it stings. I do it again and again and again with a viciousness I didn't know I contained. I feel some relief. I feel held and contained, hugged and bound.

THE POET: This is where you end and the world begins — or rather, perhaps, where the world ends and you begin.

List the Facts as They Stand:

- I have boundaries
- I am not entirely porous
- I can defend my borders
- I seek purchase
- (also)
- I carry a tiny pocketknife as a jewel on a chain around my neck

I am a vale of tears.

... on those days in which she is acceptable to herself ...

... she begins from a position of radical refusal in relation to a

system that is utterly unreformable ...

... she questions the model of solitary participant in the system, of freedom from the responsibility for other people and non-human people ...

... she resists the demeaning experience of being constantly reduced to medical diagnoses, to numbers with decimal points ...

... there is violence built into the very possibility of dialogue — of communication turned into an instrument of intimidation and terror ...

... her baseline has been in freefall for years ...

THE NANNY: Flick your rubber band, you silly girl, and come back! (This way madness lies.)

I drag myself, a little reluctantly, back from the detachment of the third person. We can accept the second person, singular. The intrusion of one voice divides a monologue into a dialogue in a symmetrical way that can be understood. The third-person address does not necessarily stop at three. It contains multitudes; in fact, it cannot be contained. It is lopsided. A third-person address is a gateway to confusion, anarchy even.

THE NANNY: Pull yourself together, Winona! Consolidate, for God's sake!

THE CHILD: Your little pieces will clog the machine!

And then when, as a young girl, I intuited what I should not know, whenever I saw a little too far in, invited uncomfortably much into the room: 'Your imagination is running away with you!'

(Whenever people said that — often — I invariably pictured Converse high-tops, sometimes red, sometimes white, but always Converse high-tops, winged like the heels of Achilles, running.)

'You are so theatrical!'

'Just be less, Winona!'

'Just. Be. Less.'

My fantasies had stopped being 'cute' at around aged eight, had become something unmanageable, a character trait that bordered even on the unseemly, a flaw just shy of vulgar. I spent hours on the school veranda as penance for my noisy disruptions of the order within.

Groupthink becomes impossible when someone uses their imagination. Imagination, intuition, critical thought is hard to police, as every repressive regime knows. Curiosity becomes a form of insubordination. This is why you kill the artists first. The more discreet, the really clever thing to do here, is to name all this thinking and feeling something else, something that can be pathologised, even criminalised, and just like that, the ground beneath your feet falls away. Now it's instability, hysteria; now manipulation, now madness, now degeneracy, now sheer lunacy. Now something dangerous to others.

You think too much.

(This is indeed a charge difficult to defend against.)

You think too much

becomes

You think the wrong thoughts

becomes

There is something wrong with you

becomes

You are wrong. Everything about you is wrong.

The germ of liberation is labelled by the organisation as a cancerous cell and chemotherapy applied.

THE ARCHER: Stop talking to yourself! There's no one there! *You assume that.*

THE SEIZURES

IT WAS A WEEKDAY during the High Dramas: the ex-husband and I were finally living in separate houses. Legally, we shared custody. I had hoped that, as I was apparently the cause of 'the problems' between the children and their father, things would improve for them all when I was not there. But the children had begun to run away on His days. The details are not important; it's enough to say the problem was not solved by removing me, and all hell rained down.

A school day, then, and I walked all the way to the bookstore because walking is one of the few things that doesn't make my shaking and my churning stomach worse. I was terrified, but there was nothing I could do except carry on putting one foot after the other. Walking felt useful and necessary: Keep Going.

Every fallen leaf in the park was brown; I closed my eyes, and the ground became a floor of eggshells. The doppler effect of a passing siren confused me — close, upon me, far.

The bushfires hadn't yet reached the cities, but every pub I limped past had its doors flung open, and their large-screen televisions beamed images of the infernos that had begun to rage all down the east coast — the cricket, and the infernos. The fires introduced themselves with a relentless push of dark air, of heat, the smell of ash, the menacing subsonic rumble ever-present under the Surface of All Things. A car skidded off at the lights and I caught a whiff of tyre smoke. The smell of burning rubber in the street always makes me afraid. There are many reasons for this.

Then I was standing in the Last Book Store Left Alive in my area, trying to escape. Reading has become more important to me than it ever was — books are the structure I can pin my days on when my mind wants to freefall. I carry at least two books with me wherever I go, and when I can't read, I listen to audio books, to music. I attempt to be in constant conversations that I actually want to be having. (Sometimes these manage to drown out the one I don't want to be having.) At nighttime, films bring temporary relief. Other people's universes become a reprieve when I cannot bear my own. Books are safety net and portal all at once, a reliable source of wonderment in a world out of control.

I remember ... I had gathered a small cairn of books and had just chosen one for my elder son. I don't remember — the smell, I do remember. It was acrid and revolting. I was back in Jakarta with that smell, driving through riots, protesters setting fire to tyres, the stench, the flames, the noise, the chaos. That was a dangerous time to be in Indonesia; I spoke little and kept my head covered and facing down. I was observing the presidential elections, and street conflicts were used as a strategy by political opponents on both sides.

Police checked the underside of every car for bombs with long slender poles affixed with mirrors. The air-conditioning grew colder, the beehives of the Indonesian Tai Tais grew ever higher and more fixed; tension banked in the humid air as the city waited for the bloodletting.

My mind was so far away — the BRIMOB men at the volcano, the Italian ambassador's party — that the shards splintered. The smell was impossible to ignore.

THE NANNY: This is happening now, not in Indonesia.

Pay attention. Indonesia is interesting, but we will look at those pieces later.

I sniffed the room, trying to locate the source of the smell. It was a smell that said:

Danger! Pay attention immediately.

Fire!

(We are all on edge from the fires.)

The man who worked in the shop — dreadlocks and large brown eyes — couldn't smell anything, nor apparently could his colleague, a sleeping marmalade cat.

I insisted.

'The air conditioning must be melting down! The electricals are short circuiting!'

No one else could smell anything. I was almost retching from the power of it. I turned towards the open door and lost consciousness.

I woke up and there had been a leap in time and space; a gap had opened. I was on a stretcher. The kind man with the dreadlocks was visible through the open doors of an ambulance, I saw that right away. The marmalade cat was not. I decided it was better not to try to force an understanding of the situation. I had nowhere to begin.

I was in the back of an ambulance. The paramedic in blue overalls was younger than I would have imagined a paramedic could be, a girl not long out of school even. She was efficient, reassuring, kind. I closed my eyes. My finger was pinched by a peg that read my heartrate. Its pressure was comforting. Nothing hurt, really. My head a little ... My hip a little ... The paramedic told me that I'd had a seizure: I blacked out and convulsed on the floor. I hadn't hit my head on the shelf, which was fortunate.

(The seizure has not been caused by my enlarged heart. Dr McAlister the cardiologist (waiting room full of goldfish; distractingly handsome in a Lawrence-of-Arabia-taking-Aqaba-type way) has since been consulted: no, my cardiomegaly is not a possible factor. This is a matter distinct and of the brain, not the heart. But really, does such a distinction exist?)

There was a stay in hospital. The dreadlocked man left a gift with my things: *Hotel du Lac* by Anita Brookner. His sensitivity slayed me.

ON THE CLIFFS

THE WIND HAS SOOTHED itself somewhat, perhaps gathering its dispersed energies for the next push. I need to leave the house and the noise of its memories: I will take advantage of the break in the wild air, and I will also take the newest poinsettia with me.

The late-morning sky remains the colour of milk, indistinct and undecided, streaked with brown. It is as if the great Sky Lord has forgotten to roll out the day's backdrop, and I am looking up at the verso of the universe. Gifted with keen eyes and a specially acquired knowledge, you can discover the history of a painting from studying its underside. In another life, I am that detective of the long-past, seeking traces of what was once lived. But today's canvas is unreadable. There are no clouds, no snatches of blue — even the dependable sun is obscured by a pale, smoky haze, making itself felt by a radiating heat, a hardboiled egg wrapped in the corner of a dirty napkin.

A solitary sulphur-crested cockatoo attempts to fly, then thinks better of it and settles back down on a power line sagging between two wooden poles, settles amongst the other cockatoos roosting there, as big as neighbourhood cats. They cackle at him like drunks at the pub and move their yellow crests wildly up and down.

(I shield my eyes from the flat, blistering light, the Bedouin seeking signs of an oasis.)

Not birds, actually. More like dinosaurs, small dinosaurs left over from a time when the world was theirs. *Archaeopteryx* —

first known bird — lived 150 million years ago. Look at them — beaks of curved horn the size of a hand, scaly legs, claws, the knowing eye ... This is no bird.

(And don't even mention cassowaries.)

The cockatoos still a rare moment and stare back, heads to one side, seven single eyes blaze unblinking. Their intelligence makes them particularly suited to living amongst humans: they can mimic human voices and have learned to open the bin lids on rubbish night. Then a motorcycle backfires, and they are off again, cackling and screeching like the tiny theropods they were not so long ago.

Apparently, humans who wake to birdsong each morning are fundamentally happier than those who don't. It is connected to feelings of safety: songbirds fall silent when predators are about. Research has been done. In England. Did cockatoos count as birds, their screams as song? It is not a relaxing sound. Even the pretty, multicoloured lorikeets — so sweet! — swarm human balconies in great flocks to screech for honey and seeds, clinging to exposed brick with tiny backward-facing claws as if it were bark, knocking at the windows with their beaks, deafening breakfast-eaters. Does that count? When my boy was a toddler, we were out rambling in a wooded section of the Great Park. Flocks of great yellow-tail black cockatoos were in the pines, tearing them apart and making a huge racket. My boy looked up at me, eyes like saucers: 'Mamma, the tree is yelling at us.'

The tree is yelling at us. Because if we could not see the cockatoos — did not know about them — maybe that is exactly what we would think: that the trees are screaming. Maybe they are.

Below today's cockatoos, a group of surfers has formed a smile on the rocks, looking out to sea, watching the swells of the ocean — cathedrals of dirty glass now — smash themselves on the base of the cliffs and then remake themselves in one sucking motion. The intake of breath, the outtake, the ocean a giant lung, breathing for us all, each wave hissing.

It's not forever, it's forever.

I sit on the grass at the top of the cliffs, in the lee of a sandstone boulder, and place the poinsettia gently beside me. The air wanders among her leaves and she looks like she is dancing.

The horizon offers some orientation on this white day. My eyes slide along its faint blue-brown curve, seeking purchase, and the certainty that the circle both begins and completes itself right here, to become Our Earth.

A tiny tanker slides along as if on rails, moving without moving; below it, a subduction zone with the deepest trenches in the world that — with active volcanoes — form the 'Ring of Fire': the Mariana, the Tonga, the Philippine, the Kuril-Kamchatka, all nudging 11,000 metres. The Mariana trench is deeper than Mount Everest is high, and if you suddenly materialised on the dark, frigid trench floor, the pressure would instantly compact your body to the size of a tin can.

I picture a pyramid stack of Warhol's Campbell's soup cans, all with the faces of people I don't wish to know. It disturbs something inside me — slight nausea — and I cast the images out.

The breeze purrs and curls through my head like white noise now, and I feel him before I see him: Bruce.

He settles next to me and follows my gaze out to sea, his mobile nose working.

BRUCE: Have you thought about what we discussed, Winona?

'To be honest, Bruce, I can't quite work it out.'

BRUCE: Don't try so hard. It will work itself out. The world was made to be free in.

Now I gently stroke the red, red leaves of the dancing poinsettia; now I lift my fingers and make the shadow profile of a rabbit, distinct even in the murky sunlight, foreshortened by the high angle of the sun, but clearly a rabbit. Thinnest of puppets, it looks about, animated, a creature possible only in the absence of itself. There is no rabbit, only my hand, but in the other world there is a playful rabbit who scratches his ear and twitches his nose and looks this way and that for danger.

This shadow rabbit absorbs all colour and light — any yearnings or subtle emotions — and becomes pure contour, receding not into darkness but into light. Its blackness is both material and immaterial: the rabbit is there; the rabbit cannot be there. His shape is part of a larger darkness: the blackness of nights without stars, of windowless rooms; the darkness of shut-eye and the blackness within our heads. The shadow twitches its ears, and suddenly we are connected to a collective memory that began with the first fire in the first cave, to a field of remembering that differs from ordinary experience, to a greater darkness — hence its power.

Shadow is both pure and impenetrable surface, and doorway to an alternative self or more radical Other, a being living a separate life, helping — often perhaps haunting — its owner.

In the world of shadows, outline is all, shape transforming with a gesture into something else entirely. Shadows are part of both the light that creates them and the object that blocks the light and allows them to be seen. They adhere to the object, extend from it, stretch, foreshorten, grow powerful at dusk and at dawn, when the veil is naturally thinnest. Shadows are the reminders of Night during the day — the remainders of the night — reminders of other places and other possibilities for happiness, even perhaps for dancing. (There are Gateway Elements, and the shadows are one.)

The children love shadow puppets; we make them on the wall with the bedside lamp, we stretch long into sunsets towards things we might not otherwise touch, we dance as elves or elephants … Sometimes, I do voices, too.

Duality: in the truth of every light-blasted day there lies another truth, thrown in black abstractions onto walls and streetscapes, that speaks of permanent and transcendental powers otherwise invisible. These shadows survive in daylight as the shards — glimpses — of an unbroken wholeness, of the implicate order of Universal Oneness, wholeness, of the interconnected fabric that is Us and the Universe. It is the darkness that is common to us all, not the divisive jumble of day-shapes that define us and make us distinct from one another. The shadow joins us to a shared darkness, and to something that is already inside each of us. Obscurity can join us in a way that the light cannot.

Where the light is blocked, there is another world that is possible: the shadows show a truer thing.

BRUCE: The shape of your own absence is casting a shadow right there near the rock, next to mine.

I reach out my shadow rabbit, transform it into a bird, and lightly peck at Bruce's shadow ear. Day-Bruce turns to me, and Night-Bruce becomes a dragon, my bird a retreating snake.

BRUCE: Shadow is universal to All Things, even mountains. It is a bringing forth of the things ordinarily kept hidden.

BRUCE: (The ear must be itched.)

'Of course. Please continue when you're ready.'

BRUCE: The shadow is an emanation of something within us: to cast a different shadow, you must first change your shape.

'I don't want to cast a shadow; I want to be invisible.'

BRUCE: Have you ever tried to shake your shadow?

I shake my head.

BRUCE: In times of crisis, the shadow is your witness. The night has eyes to recognise its own.

He pees softly on the grass.

BRUCE: (The compulsion here is strong.)

He settles back beside me, and I rest my hand on his back. It helps me focus on his thoughts.

'I think it takes courage to allow yourself to be visible to others, and not in one of those clever, complicated ways in which we mimic being present when really we're not there. I am searching for this courage every day.'

BRUCE: If you're visible, you can be seen, you can be touched, you can be hurt. It's a choice you make to be vulnerable in this true way. It is both a superpower and a deeply human one.

'What do you know of being human, Bruce?' (gently).

BRUCE: I know their ways; I study them when they do not know they are visible. That is my advantage. Their masks mean nothing to me. I see differently. I sense them, I smell them, I hear them, I watch them move with others through the day. I know which is kind to animals, which one will shout at children, which one feels like a desolate wanderer on the surface of a moon. I can chart the topography of their pain with my nose. The human heart is a complicated organ and can be wounded in so many subtle ways. It can also love in so many subtle ways.

'But you have language for this.'

BRUCE: You have the language. I am telegraphing to you my thought-forms. Your mind is pinning them to words that you can understand. It's quite simple, really.

'We communicate like tap roots.'

BRUCE: Perhaps that is one way to give the sensation a corresponding and concrete shape ... It's both song and science.

There is a pause as he brings his back leg up to scratch his ear again. My mind fills with his dandelions, with the dandelions and weeds growing all around us.

BRUCE: You humans can refuse to be yourselves. Herein lie the layers of complication. The tree cannot refuse to be anything but a tree, the cloud cannot, the waves cannot. The tree is simply tree-ing, the cloud is cloud-ing, the waves are wave-ing. This is why they comfort your turbulent heart. They cannot but fully inhabit their elemental nature. As I cannot but fully inhabit mine.

He looks up the street for a long time, his nose twitching now with purpose.

'Bruce?'

BRUCE: Seek the people who bring you alive.

'You bring me alive.'

BRUCE: Now you are simply rubbing me in butter.

'It is a nice thing ...'

BRUCE: You must get used to living like a tree. No bird sings-ish, no plant grows-ish. They pursue wholeheartedly their endeavour — to melodise, to push green — purely because it is enough.

'I contend with stealth expectations and attendant dis-appointments. There are weighted silences. I seek profound progress of the soul.'

BRUCE: Yes. How can you expect that this comes as easily as walking?

'Yes. You are right.'

Silence and now the mind fills with ocean, with smoke, with the smell of hot, dry soil, of eucalypts.

The voices of the surfers catch a gust and drift up to us in snatches.

'Check out that set!'

'Is that a fucking shark, mate?!'

'Nah. Dolphin —?'

'Kelp, I reckon —'

Their sulphur crests, bleached by sun and salt, rise and fall too.

'We mimic the world around us, unwittingly.'

BRUCE: Then you should choose your place carefully, Winona.

'What if you don't have a choice?'

BRUCE: Then you must adapt to the environmental conditions or die. It's Darwinian.

'I have Things to Say about Darwin.'

I stroke the grass, pull gently on its brittle blades.

'He never intended his discovery to pit species against species. Darwin studied Buddhism and beauty and saw the compassion in our nature ... His theory was interpreted to turn life into a competitive arena of blood from which a victor would emerge —'

BRUCE: From which an Uber-human would emerge —

'He wrote "survival of the fit" not "the fittest". It makes a difference. I seek conviviality, emotional reciprocity.'

BRUCE: When thinking about evolution, you might consider

also the role of genius loci, the nexus of the geography of the body and the geography of place — smells, landforms, story — that creates something unique to you.

'Without doubt this is a force that can neither be discounted nor resisted —'

Fresh cries tear the air. Not the long, large vowels of before: short-sharp this time, urgent.

'Over there! Over there!!'

The surfers are pointing now, all of them, out to sea. A great brown wave passes below the cliff, carrying the body of a surfer, face down. Black wetsuit, board gone, he rises and falls with each set, splayed on the ocean's chest like a soft marionette. Beside him — the surfers point — the too-smooth lip of a rip that will shoot him to New Zealand.

(To gentle death.)

On the beach, Surf Rescue has also seen the surfer, and the red zodiac with its powerful caged propellor comes racing out. The red-and-yellow figures gather and clump, yellow boards at the ready; a siren keens in the distance.

Time here is the difference between triumph and disaster. Fold the cloths of time, and you make room for millions of possibilities from a single moment. Time's linear forward momentum as understood by humans is the violence that undoes us.

Fold the cloths of time! Save that man! Pause it!

The waves suck then swallow the base of the cliffs, creating a rhythm that is felt rather than heard — felt in the upper chest, in the blood — glassy heaves and shrugs indifferent to the drama of humans. Nature makes no distinction between lost lives ungrievable and those worthy of sorrow. It is humans who decide whether to grieve a life or withhold that grief — eat the lamb, mourn the child, cut the tree, kill the murderer, save the old lady at all costs. Who is what to whom in all our billions of separate universes? Like folds in the cloths of time, all possibilities exist at once until sheared by exposure to human time. All yesterdays are tomorrows.

Like Schrödinger's cat, all possible outcomes are true until the box is opened ...

(What is this human obsession with opening doors and boxes and caves that should stay closed?! Bluebeard, the tombs of Egypt ...)

THE NANNY: DO NOT OPEN THE BOX, PANDORA-WINONA.

My mind wants to cave in, and it's only noon.

Focus on the surfer, pray. Save this man.

It's not forever, but it's forever.

They have dragged the soft surfer from the water. On the beach now, they start chest compressions.

BREATHE!

I hear the distant shout from the lifeguards, a command to a man with lungs that won't start:

BREATHE!

The blue light from the sand buggy strobes the pale face of the surfer, stroking it blue.

Someone yelled that when my baby was born blue, water on the lungs:

'Breathe, baby, breathe!'

I had whispered it to myself, knees folded under like an origami bird, one wing over each boy, willing the sick shaking fear to subside, willing a hedge of protection from His storm:

— breathe, baby, breathe.

This is how love ends. This is the point of carelessness where Love is now forever filed under Lost Things.

A man kneels by the surfer's head and gives the kiss of life. Suddenly he convulses, and they roll him onto his side; he vomits up the sea. Land reclaims its primacy, claims the position of Foremost in the surfer's life today.

We are always on the brink of losing everything, and the possibility of winning it all back. It is what makes life bearable — the hope! — and unbearable at the same time. We can spend a lifetime trying to embrace The Unknown, to make friends with the fact that we have no idea what will come next. And it will never fully happen, this rapprochement; we will never be completely comfortable with Not Knowing. We set our little habits — order our shoes, walk clockwise around the park, fill our calendars with precise reminders for an imagined future. But when we look long enough into the void, these microscopic buttresses fall away, and we feel the void — to echo Nietzsche, that metaphysician of fear — looking into us. And it is in the striving to give it form that we create the purpose, the magic we need, to keep on living: we make art, we make babies; we build tunnels and skyscraper and rockets and entertainment units to convince ourselves. We shout, we fuck, we fight, we gamble, we pray, we get high; we develop a tolerance, perhaps, and perhaps that is the best we can do.

We can learn to find pleasure in the contemplation of 'terrible' things: objects too vast, too deep, too big, too dark to be fully comprehended. The intimidation of the wholly uncontrollable creates a duality of pleasure and terror in the brain of the beholder. Edmund Burke called this 'the Sublime', and the world went giddy with the idea of it.

The earth makes and unmakes itself in every instance. Stones and rocks only seem permanent in relation to our mutability — geologically, stone is as defenceless to transformation as any other substance. It is only a matter of Time. The waves understand this as they break, roll in, claim space, roll back; every wave redefines the boundary of the sea, the limits of the land. The sea takes all forms and holds none. To understand the rhythms of the world, you have only to watch waves breaking, or maybe clouds. Clouds also carry the ephemeral notion that they are always clouds but never the same cloud. They, too, make wild shapes yet hold none. They, too, are water but never the same stream.

It's not forever; it's forever.

A woman comes sprinting across the sand from far off. She stumbles many times, and from this I know it is his wife, his lover, coming to find him. That question, surely — *what if it's not forever and this is forever?* Another ghost caught in the throat. Her focus is motion, this she can do; close the space between her and her beloved.

The rescuers have the surfer on a board now; the paramedics arrive. There is an oxygen mask on his face. The woman reaches him and bends her head in love over his, to let him know she is there. They leave the shore and begin to run with the board to the ambulance waiting on the promenade, its doors flung open to receive them.

At their backs, the sea surges and retreats, a fault line shifting shape with every breath. There are no red-and-yellow flags marking the safe place to swim today, only poles with yellow signs that say **DANGEROUS CURRENT**, the black stick figure of a swimmer in the waves run through with a red X. All lines, says the sea, are arbitrary. All opposites encircle to meet their ends. And like the woman stooped over her lover's pale face, love bends.

Serpent, tooth, tail.
Love bends to hate, bends to love.

(BRUCE KNOWS THE STORY of the Poinsettia Rescue. Here is what happened not long after we moved into the new house.)

I might have walked on. But I didn't do that. I can only plead an avian enchantment, perhaps, a sort of hypnosis ... The events that followed could not be attributed entirely to my actions alone. If I were breaking down a film script for a client, we might call the bird the 'inciting element' — the inciting incident. Everything flowed from the moment my day intersected with that of the bird. Simply put:

girl meets bird/bird meets girl

— and we have the nub of the cause, the germ of the seed, the beginning of the road that led to the Police.

This road, leading from my new house, is constantly in some state of repair or disrepair. It has become a walkway, scarred all over — irresistible slabs of fresh cement! — with graffiti: initials, love hearts pierced by arrows, names, the imprint of a fallen flower. Our initials too, on a small wet edge, the first three letters of our names and a love heart with wings. (For the first time I noticed the edge of a large paw print — Bruce's? Had it always been there or miraculously manifested itself in the dry cement via a loop in time and space, a tear in the cosmic cloth?)

This road also has a neglected house halfway down, an overgrown lot, a dark brick bungalow with a padlock on the rotting timber garage. Number 154. Perhaps it's home to squatters or a shut-in, or perhaps it's simply abandoned. The front garden is a roil of grass and leaves, set apart from the neighbours' houses with their gravelled paths and surfboard racks, their covered barbeques and perfectly clean garages filled with large, busy cars and the evidence of Sport.

I saw two girls climb out of the window there one morning, but they didn't look like they belonged to the house; they didn't use the door. The most interesting thing about this house, however, is The Bower.

Hidden by a shrub and tucked into the long grass, there is a cathedral of twigs almost a metre high, built by a bower bird. The structure is a small study in miracles. It is built in the shape of two cresting waves, facing each other, spume-tips touching. The tunnel-form between the waves is the bower, a dark, curved space, and you can look right through to the other side. It invites you in, with its skill and evocation of wonder. I long to be small enough to enter.

The male bowerbird, unlike the splendid display of the peacock who fans out his feathers like so many $100 notes, uses the spectacle of his intelligence and creativity to attract the female. The beautiful bowers are decorated with flower petals, feathers, shells, bones, and sparkly man-made objects — sparkly or blue. The bowerbird is obsessed by the colour blue. The bower is there for luring females and mating; it is not a nest. The plain-coloured female builds a nest herself, and is left to raise her young there alone.

Last week, there had been a display of rosella feathers and blue clothes pegs, raided from a neighbouring yard, no doubt, as carefully laid out as menhirs or the shards of a broken heaven. That is also a mystery, why bowerbirds crave the colour blue — although perhaps it's not so mysterious after all: blue is the colour of the sea, the sky, all things eternal. It is the colour found at the very edge of things.

The light that gives us the colour blue is light that has gotten lost on its way to us from the sun. Its particles have shattered, and lodged in clear water and transparent air. The bowerbird's yen for blue feels like a window into his heart, and it has become my mirror. I feel kindred with the small feathery poet in the abandoned garden, with his enthusiasm for love, his capacity for melancholy, his desire for transcendence.

Blue is the most beautiful colour they know.

The bowerbird is also a magician. The bower is a House of Illusions, a place of optic transfigurations and sleights of hand (beak), all planned out to manipulate the female's perception, to lure her to spend longer and longer in the bower. The male knows that the longer a potential mate lingers in his funhouse, the likelier she is to stay forever. The research has been done here also: the male bowerbird arranges his treasures — curates them — in a way that creates a false read of the geometry of the bower.

He places the smaller objects closer to the mouth, the larger objects at a distance, so that all the objects appear the same size. The female loses her sense of perception — reality is skewed — and somehow, she is entranced. The male, during the courtship, waves certain objects at the female, making them appear larger in size, hypnotic. Researchers are not sure exactly how this enraptures the female or influences her choice, but they've recorded that if the objects are moved by human hand, the male returns and replaces them in their original position.

(I watch a man in the neighbouring driveway back a Porsche SUV with the greatest care into a very small carport, while his wife offers hand gestures to represent direction and available space, guiding him in from the open doorway. Original position.)

I like to check in and see what delights him, for I am a scavenger, too. Found objects carry a small mystical weight, as if I were *meant* to find that lost playing card — the ace of hearts! — or the lock that had no hole for a key, or the small silver hand grenade, the pink golf ball, the piece of glass worn down by the waves into the shape of a heart. My pocket litter; his Cave of Wonders.

On that day, it was his song that found me first. It started as a buzzing, an electronic pulse reverberating at high speed, churning, whirring like a lightsabre. It's not the sound you expect from any bird, any creature. And yet, the bowerbird can mimic anything: the barking of a dog, a human coughing, the thwack of an axe chopping wood, children playing, a car alarm ... Any female bowerbird would be impressed that her potential mate can hold a universe in his throat.

The wonderbird was there, busy, fluffing his feathers. I crouched at what I hoped was a respectful distance and peered in. The bird made a great fluff of his wings, filling the daylight space with his feathers, blocking the light, before dashing out and disappearing. I had disturbed him, and for this I was sorry. His cathedral was unattended.

I looked for traces of what the morning had held for him: two silver bottle caps, half a blue biro, and a blue chewing-gum wrapper; further down, a more solid flash of blue, rectangular. The markings on it caught my attention and I peered closer ... A bright blue key tag with the word 'Caretaker' in black, attached to an old-fashioned silver key.

I slowed down to consider: a caretaker's key. In the nest. No doubt thieved from a local door. The audacity thrilled me, a stolen key, a burglar bird — possibilities yet unexplored were begging, *begging*, to be set in motion.

Like the bower-hen I was enchanted. As I said, I can only blame enchantment for what happened next. As slow as a stalking cat, I inched my hand towards the key, violating the bird's privacy, daring myself, aware of the disrespect and yet compelled. The compulsion to take the key could not be denied.

With my other hand, I searched in my pocket for an abandoned treasure I half-remembered was there: the Matchbox car. It was silver with bright-blue racing stripes. A fine exchange.

I took the key. Then I reached back in and carefully placed the car in its stead. Not a robbery; a swap.

I pocketed the key, again resisting the urge to move furtively.

(We are compelled to respond to and replicate that which we are most awed by in nature.)

It was a natural progression of the story then to spot, soon after, the blue door with the old-fashioned lock. Walking a route I walk daily, I wondered I hadn't remarked it before: a ground floor door at the bottom of a crumbly block of flats popular with Brazilian travellers looking for cheap rooms near the sea. It was too serendipitous for it not to Be.

The front window was dark and fly-blown, the grass around the concrete path too long. No blinds, no curtains, no caretaker. A roll of dead carpet lay on the grass outside.

I walked to the front door. I knew with a cosmic certainty that should I slide the key into the lock it would turn ... I was meant to find it and to know exactly where it belongs.

I felt no qualms, but I tried the door handle before I tried the key: the door was unlocked.

I pushed the sticky, flimsy door and crossed a threshold.

```
INT. APARTMENT — DAY

The apartment is abandoned, dusty, and empty
of furniture. A drying rack and a broken
phone sit on the kitchen counter. The linoleum
floor is bubbling and peeling, the counters
stained, but it is otherwise unremarkable.

WINONA, slender, furtive, enters the room …
```

I poke around, the stillness and silence thrilling me. The moment feels stolen, secret, safe. Pleasurably strange. Two tiny bedrooms with windows onto the innards of a lantana bush, dark and tangled; a living room; a small bathroom with a rust-stained tub. So many lives lived here, and yet no real trace of what has been before.

Time/transience.

On the windowsill in the kitchen, the sole survivor of the exodus, a poinsettia plant, a casualty from last Christmas most likely, sits alone, leaf-tips browning, too warm, too thirsty. We lock Beings, the poinsettia telegraphing a message of distress right to my receiver, so exquisitely attuned to that frequency.

Before thoughts can form, I cross the linoleum, lift the poinsettia, and place it in the sink. I run the dribbly tap, slake its thirst, then pivot and stride purposefully out of the front door with the plant, the flowerpot leaking mud onto my arm. I close the door carefully behind me and leave the key on the mat.

This is not the first plant I have rescued, but it is the first I have recovered in an illegal raid on someone's home.

It is a beginning, not an end.

ON THE GRASSY CLIFFTOP by the sea, the wind is picking up and the surfers have gone. The surfer's rescue from drowning is a beginning not an end; the poinsettia's rescue —

What else might be done that has been heretofore left undone?

The possibilities silence us all — plant/ dog/ human. I think of Louise Bourgeois' needles, her repairs: doing, undoing, redoing.

The moment is ripe for thoughts to blow in, fetid and tugging. Bruce's fur ripples unevenly. Windy days must be so intense for him, his body covered in hair, pulled this way and that, tickled all over — drive him mad, surely ... He remains, however, unmoved, and I wonder what wind unfolded him that he can be so patient, so good. The trees here grow small and stunted, bonsaied by ocean gales, but vigorous. They catch light, accept the rain, and use their silent magical powers to transform both into food.

I envy them their ability to photosynthesise.

The things we want are transformative. Blue is this for the bowerbird, perhaps the plants for me. I want to learn from their gentle striving. They bend in a gale, throw roots into the rocky cracks, they take the shape of the wind. They persist.

We must get used to living like a bush, a tussock, a tree.

I stretch my fingers and feel the air rush through them like velvet.

I am seeking a rejuvenation of our carnal, sensorial empathy with the living land that sustains us.

A glance at the liberated poinsettia, also feeling the breeze, revelling, it pleases me to consider, in its freedom from the hot flat.

A finger of unease plucks some unseen interior string.

THE ARCHER: You are stealing from people's houses.

Yes. (Sorry.)

THE NANNY: You could put it back. You could return the plant to where you found it.

THE POET: No! You can't rebottle feelings! You can't Take It Back. None of it. When you touch the world, it touches you back, and everything is irrevocably changed. It's not how it was before.

THE CHILD: No one saw you —

THE POET: The world watches us! We walk through a forest of eyes every day, all the other perceivers — animals, birds, plants, a lifeworld, the common field of our lives.

I glance sideways at the poinsettia, the evidence of all wrongdoing squatting happily beside me in mute loyalty, complicit.

THE ARCHER: From now on, every siren you hear will be coming for you.

Yes.

I stroke the grass to reassure it.

THE POET: Every gesture is the bodying-forth of emotion. It has been written.

THE NANNY: Is that why you stole the plant? Your emotions momentarily took over? I fear for you.

It's more imperative than that. The body and its sensations are how the outside world invades us, and the ways we have of meeting this invasion.

THE CHILD: You make it sound like a war.

No. It's not a war. A porous interplay of energies to be accepted as elemental. It does not become a war until this acceptance is branded demonic, until it is heresy to acknowledge the intelligence of the body, of instinct, until knowing is alienated from being. Who we are and what we know are divorced —

(THE NANNY: That word is unsafe territory. Step back. Breathe. Begin again.)

(pause)

Tens of thousands of women were tortured and killed in 300 years. It was enough for a woman to show a love of animals, or to walk alone in the fields to be called a witch. The women were killed for allowing the wind, and the world is out of balance because of it.

THE ARCHER: You would have been tortured and killed.

(I know.)

PATHOLOGY

BACK HOME, I RETURN the poinsettia to her place among the other plants. Sometimes when I water them, the morning sun streams in horizontally to bathe the leaf tips in gold, and it becomes a cathedral, and I could cry with the glory of it.

This is not my home. Or rather, I have rented a clean, solid house near the school: compact, concrete, impenetrable. It looks from the outside a little like a white machine-gun bunker. Inside, it is boxy and white and has too many cables; the walls are punctured with power-points, and cords and flexes snake from them, run behind appliances, slither along skirting boards before disappearing into another mysterious hole. It is unclear what they are for but also very clear that one must not touch or investigate lest we skew some electronic equilibrium and are plunged into a technological chaos I have little faith I could find my way back from.

Telepathy and intuition have been replaced by electronic communication devices that require complicated cabling in the physical world so we can reach the virtual one.

Moon is the oldest TV.

In this cabled house, things happen on their own: lights go on at certain times; at other times, blinds lower themselves over west-facing windows that catch a scorching bowlful of the summer-evening sun. There is a light switch labelled **Goodbye** that plunges the entire house into darkness; there is a lot of construction in the streets during the day, and a lot of bins being dragged, skateboards, bongo drumming, shouting, mysterious Bangs in the night. It can sometimes feel as if the poltergeists are in charge.

I don't mind it. None of it is unfriendly, just curious. There are high concrete walls on all sides crowned with a vigorous bougainvillea that explodes in vivid fuchsia clusters. Mostly, the house is a huge relief. I am grateful to it. It is a protected place where we can feel safe.

I gather the rescue plants — amputees, refugees, veterans; the unwanted, the unclaimed, the unearthed — to soften the edges of the rooms and to bring Life and Air. I leave my one beautiful painting propped against the kitchen wall, unhung, and add layers of carpets, cushions. I want to feel like a nomad passing through this house; it isn't my place, and it doesn't feel like it could be mine. I am tentative yet. I lack the solidity and certainty to put down roots. I am not ready to solidify from my liquid state — my fluxus — as Things That Need to Change are still changing, and I need that to keep happening.

By committing to wind and water, and then to the Flow of Things, I feel I am protecting space for transformation. When He moved out from our shared home and took the Stuff, gaps were created that, even here, I'm not ready to fill. I need to notice how temporary my dining table is — a smooth wooden door placed on builders' sawhorses, and covered in a pale blue patterned cloth; I need to notice that I have no coffee table books, that my lovely vases are gone, that I have only my single beautiful painting, that our bedside tables are made of upturned milk crates ... I need to feel His absence every day. Perhaps that makes no sense and masks a reluctance to commit; perhaps it is a way of maintaining hope. Likely, it is both.

Like the glacier: a permanent state of flux. Paradox is possible, even necessary. It is, in fact, a prerequisite for true freedom.

Hope is not inexhaustible — its source must be nourished; certain conditions must be maintained for it to continue burning. When we first moved in, a tendril crept in from the outside, as if to say hello, to confound the categories of Inside and Outside. The window stayed ajar all winter to make space for the tendril. It is a passionflower vine, and it has now begun to run over the wall to frame the kitchen sink.

I sense a restlessness among the plants today and stand as still as I can, allowing them to fully sense me. I have been practising Telepathic Receptivity: it takes the form of a constant yet indistinct focus. It is a bit like conjuring fog or directing clouds in a very intentional way. I must concentrate intensely and yet define nothing, seek no fixed points. I find it takes a fierce and concerted effort to do this — to thin the veil — that often leaves me exhausted, a little dizzy even. To hold space loosely, gently, to dissolve the categories between us, I let the sounds of the wind rush through my mind, I patient ... I nebulise ... The process is a bit like tuning a radio: the messages often burst, truncate, or fade, softly overlap, blur around their edges. When I can make a clear energetic connection, the plant-voices are polyphonic, with two, three, four, five heard at the same time, independent melodies working on top of each other yet protected from blending into monophony by the etiquette of crown shyness. I think of their emanations as 'songs', because I don't have another word to convey how deeply they move me, how something about their energetic discharge shakes important things loose far inside. I think of the Sardinian *Cantu a Tenore* singers, the Corsicans, the Leelo of Estonia, the African mushroom gatherers ... I close my eyes and become a cosmos stretching backwards and forwards into All Time, for one short moment, I am completely whole. My mind tunes in:

THE PLANTS: Vanish in pieces to protect the whole; they cannot kill what they cannot find

All is wind and water

We are the frequency holders, the emanators of peace and stillness, the contemplative ones

There is no room for us in your society

We are pushed out by the noise.

(Yes.)

THE PLANTS: There are things you need to hear.

(Yes. I am here.)

THE PLANTS: Devotion begins with close attention

Attention with feeling differs from observation

Circles of compassion widen

It is from the damage that we grow

The crushing and the cutting.

I am working hard to repair what has been done, and undone, and done again.

THE PLANTS: The effort to repair effervesces with energy. Something 'third' emerges, not what was before

Not the broken

A third state

Resilience is the third state

Our resurrection is birthed on the field of our demise. That is where you have to look.

My days have no form.

THE PLANTS: Wind is your possibility — striving after wind is an expression of your wildness and refusal to conform

Every time the wind moves through you, you travel with it
Wind is breath and speech and movement and tenderness
Wind is destiny
Wind is the world moving through you.
(Breathe, baby.)

THE PLANTS: Trust yourself in treading lightly enough to fly if you must
The earth has scorched your feet
Attend carefully
Allow the wind.

THE POET: The spiderwebs refract the sun after rain, the maharani dons her pearls; the skies pass on the light-messages of dead stars. Look at me. See this. I am here but not here, all at the same time. I am in constant motion, I circle your optical nerve you pupil your eyeball the earth. I resist squares like the wind, like the water, light, like you.

THE PLANTS: Your loyalty to this must be as total as water's commitment to gravity, as total as the sun's vow to ever-passage the sky
Seek the Thin Places.

The clockface a silver-white spider egg with spider's legs — sixty minutes, twelve times five, luminous displays, the numbers tick forwards, tick forwards then repeat.

I want to live outside human time. It is the time of minerals and mountains that interests me.

THE NANNY: I understand. However, there is an appointment to attend at noon, and it will remain there to be attended no matter how far you travel from the ordinary world.

Right.

THE NANNY: The portal has closed. It is best you begin walking now.

THE ARCHER: Best you begin walking now.

On the street, bin lids have opened in the updrafts. Rubbish flies unevenly, sprints and eddies, catching on branches and lampposts and the handlebars of bicycles.

I move slowly, but with purpose. One foot in front of the other will eventually get you anywhere.

When the Westerly winds blow hot and dry from the desert heart of the country, they bring with them a giddiness that — in someone Sensitive to Phenomena Natural and Otherwise — can manifest as madness. The day my second son was born, there was a dust storm. No fires, but great clouds of red sand like monstrous billowing skyscrapers, like the skyline of a new and expanding city massing above our own. I believe in auguries — not as predestination or fate, but rather as an acknowledgment of Other. Fixating on the unknowable and the improbable is my way of praying, my way of creating gaps in the known — cracks — in which there is room for possibility, holding a space for mystery.

The storm had raged for days and by his birthday in October, the fiery sand had all but blotted out the sun, and we moved in twilight. Eight years ago.

We stretched through the half-light with scarves wound around our nose and mouth; we washed our flowers in the hope that they could still breathe, but the water made the red sand run and it looked like blood. Schools closed, and people stayed indoors with their curtains drawn, nursing headaches, and asthma, and streaming eyes. No view was temporarily worth anything in the wealthy waterside suburbs. Leaves withered and fell and were carried with the sand across the sky, replacing all the birds that would not fly. Skeins tangled and nerves pulled tight. There was a fear palpable in shops, in dust-creased faces — conversations turned to the Old Testament and a vengeful god, to plagues and unexplained phenomena that can also be called disasters; to arks built in a hurry, and withered plants, and blood and blight.

Sunsets were wild and fierce, the sky cycling through oranges and pinks and desperate reds, lowering itself over the city, a snow-globe of sand. The desert was moving to the town, as all nomads know it eventually does. This is why they keep moving. I think of the Rub' al Khali — the desert of the 'Empty Quarter' on the Arabian Peninsula — of the reddish-orange dunes that stretch for 650,000 square kilometres, of the tribes who move there: the Al Murrah, the Banu-Yam, the Banu Hamdan, the Bani Yas ...

One day, when I was reading more about these desert tribes, I came across an article describing the discovery of a 'nomad' or 'Wanderlust' gene. It is known as DRD4-7R, and is apparently linked to dopamine that provokes divergent ideas and renders settled life a misery for those who have it; it has them seeking horizons as for water, for air. If that were true, what might that mean for people who were unknowingly living the wrong life for their DRD4-7R traits? Nomad, from 'nomas', people who are not known. Nomads, who have trodden lightly on the earth and left no roads or ruins, no cathedrals, tombs and monuments; no libraries, only songs. Their life is lived just over the horizon: they are always just about to arrive.

THE POET: Sehnsucht.

Yes, Sehnsucht. My perpetual state: longing, desire, yearning, craving for some invisible, ideal alternative experience, one that colours all the unfinished and imperfect aspects of my day.

Our happiness dwells in this space of anticipation.

THE NANNY: You surely possess the DRD4-7R. The blood nurse should test you for this.

Yes. I could well do. Out of place, out of time, out of genetic concert with my surroundings.

(THE POET: Make a small rotation, face the sun, and the shadows fall away.)

My grandfather the explorer once told me that desert people fear blue eyes: if you hold a skull to the sky, blue fills the socket. Blue eyes mean death. His eyes were a brilliant blue; my eyes are blue too, deeper, though, sometimes bruising to violet. The desert will not run out. It will creep to invade the cities we place — great hubris — around its edges; the stars will not run out — the sky is blind without them.

(I could have read the omen then, but I did not. I left it lying like an unpaid bill in an unopened envelope by the door.)

I do remember the small smooth dunes of red sand — so soft — that had banked against the gutters and built up on the footpaths, on the corners of buildings, the doorways of real estate agents and fried chicken shops … I imagined the dunes building up and up, reclaiming the hair salons and nail bars, the juice bars and cafes. I thought of it at night, lying on my side with a pillow between my knees, heavy and restless with my unborn son curled in my belly; I stroked the tiny feet that pummelled visibly — restless, too — under my skin and thought of swathes of sand, of a sea of dunes rising and cresting over the buildings in my street. It became a form of meditation, a vision so soothing in its impermanence.

In one dimension of time, this is already a ruined city.

I always imagined it would be the ocean that would reclaim us, but perhaps it will be the sand that turns green plains brown, silts rivers, buries our cars, settles softly over us while we sleep.

Pompeii.

The wind pulled at my threads. My baby was coming.

I have a photo I took of a rose garden while I was out walking in the early hours of my labour, when the wincing pangs were still ignorable. The roses are white — were white, you can spot the creamy winks in the under-folds of the flowers — but in the photo, they are burnt orange and matt from the dust. Plastic bags are caught and shredded on the thorns; the sky behind is dark, pink and grey and brown.

My mind the rubbish-strewn hedge. No ordinary day this, the day my baby was born with water on his lung.

THE WALK TO THE appointment is long and hot, and the wind is not at my back. I spit grit and keep my sunglasses on against the flying debris. I could have called an Uber, but I don't want to get there any faster. I pass a bungalow with several plants dying on a kitchen windowsill. My fingers tingle.

THE NANNY: The elastic bands around your biceps!
THE POET: Their frequency emanation!
Both.

I want to take them with me. My canvas bag is big enough to hold all the plants ... My feet dance back and forth; I cannot move on and yet —

A woman and a toddler are in the shade of the doorway, playing with a plastic tub of water, a cup. It is their house.

THE NANNY: The moment is now or never. Seize it!

I wave at them. I try to sound chirpy, like the slightly over-involved but generally harmless neighbour who pops over in sitcoms. I smile, and I point, and I cry: 'Oh, how lovely to play with water on such a hot day!! I think your plants are thirsty, too!!'

The woman and child turn to me as one with large blank eyes. I wave again. I am forced to keep moving on lest the situation get weird. I hope my pearls, my smile, reassure them — not much else about me usually has that effect on strangers.

I remove the elastic bands from my biceps with some awkwardness.

I walk on.

We — (you know who you are, quite simply because this will be true for you, too) — are not invisible. We are ignored. There is a difference. The latter is an active choice to discount or leave acknowledged the effect — or even the existence of — someone or something; unless it's for purposes of tact or etiquette, it is not usually done kindly. It can be a provocation or a power play. To ignore a voice is to silence it. It is a first and necessary step to denying the existence of a human, a non-human, a problem, a first step to making sure it is fully understood that They don't matter as much as others do. Once the right to recognition has been successfully denied, the situation can either be a) reframed with a narrative better suited to the Purpose at Hand or b) erased. Damnatio memoriae, etc. As I said, we are ignored until we are not.

When I was a teenager, I read a book about how women could avoid being raped, or beaten, or killed. I was being stalked by a moonfaced man — an ex-boyfriend, older, one of the Night People who fascinated me as a high school girl. Moonface had decided, on more than one occasion, that *No* meant *Yes*. No, in fact, meant *Go for It!* (fortissimo).

I was seventeen. I didn't know what to do or how to ask for help. All the advice I could find was on how to catch a man and keep him; there was nothing on how to make one go away. I finally found a book called *The Gift of Fear* by Gavin DeBecker and read it twice. From it, I learned that any attention you give a stalker is seen as encouragement, even if it's NO, I NEVER WANT TO SEE YOU AGAIN EVER. Any answer is a positive result for them. The only thing you can do, advises Gavin DeBecker, is vanish, evade, stay silent; swallow provocations, listen to your fear, flee.

I also read that it's of little use to shout HELP! when being attacked. People do not want to be involved; HELP begs for their attention and paradoxically makes them turn away. The thing to shout instead is FIRE!

Fire is something universally agreed upon as perilous. Shouting FIRE is guaranteed to have a much greater degree of success: it offers many more opportunities for uncomplicated bravery. People will pay attention to that, run towards the possible source to see — a fire might also involve them! (This advice, too, has stayed with me.)

The waiting room at pathology is overcrowded, lines of patients standing, sitting, masked, anxious, texting. I am anxious, too. I resist the urge to resist the situation. I attempt an attitude of Radical Acceptance. Active resistance will only exhaust me, make more trouble in the end, draw the target more vividly on my back. It will make no difference to the outcome.

THE NANNY: Remember Gavin DeBecker; remember that you need to disappear; remember not to offer Him any attention, positive or negative. It is fuel to the fire.

But what about my fire? He is still trying to control my body. Why is He still allowed to hurt me? (Terror and helplessness). I despair — I can't get away from Him, I can't breathe — I'm shaking — I can't feel my legs — I can't breathe —

FIRE!

THE CHILD: It's only a panic attack. You can breathe! It's impossible to die from a panic attack. Slowly slide down the wall and sit on the floor. There are no free chairs, so it won't look weird that you're sitting on the floor.

THE NANNY: Listen to me: this is an intended consequence

on His part; this is the point. You must undergo tests to prove you are not mad. This is impossible to do. But by demanding the tests, his accusation has been medicalised and stands on record. He has weaponised your diagnosis. It has been legitimised, and you can't disprove a negative.

THE ARCHER: Just ask the thousands of women locked up in the lunatic asylums of history, lobotomised, dehumanised, driven insane by men who 'loved' them. Why are you even surprised?

THE POET: Consider this moment as a link in a chain that was forged before the burning of the witches. Let that steady your hand.

The nurse calls my name.

(fire)

In her surgery, the nurse ties a tourniquet. Its grip is oddly comforting, a tether, an embrace. (The red marks are still on my arm from the elastics, but she affects not to notice. I am embarrassed into even deeper silence.) The nurse's dark eyes are kind, her name tag suggests that perhaps she is of Iranian heritage. I focus on these details. Her fingers are not His fingers, I force myself to notice. She has clean, short, oval nails. She prepares the syringe, carefully swabs the inside of my elbow with alcohol. Her fingers are not His fingers.

'... a bit like a bee sting.'

I nod. I try to speak clearly when I ask: 'Are you having a good day?'

The nurse pauses to consider this. The question feels odd, she is right, but I am trying to talk to make her talk so I can reassure myself that any transmutation of his fingers into hers is imagined.

She thinks I am afraid of needles — my trembling, freezing fingers, eyes wide above my mask — and she obliges me.

'Yes, but it's very busy out there. It's always busy.'

I nod.

Misattribution.

Now the needle is pulling my blood. The test tube fills and there, capped and labelled, a deep and fancy red, is my life force. I feel slightly nauseated, lightheaded. My face tingles. The nurse asks if I'm okay. I nod.

I'm not okay, but there's nothing you or anyone else can do about it. I thank you for asking.

She peels and places a small Band-Aid on the puncture wound. I praise the deftness of her fingers, her skill with the needle. I thank her.

(I hope then that at least one of us will walk away having had a positive experience. With these small reversals, we rehearse for the possibility of greater ones.)

I hurry past the smoothie bar, the low-carb chicken wraps, avert my eyes from the man in the pointed suede boots and the short black hair brushed forward, the tight jeans and the loud voice, the lip-smacking smile of self-satisfaction —

THE CHILD: He made that bruise.

He has left impressions inside me. Not transferred tastes but rather their opposite — aversions. Almond mylk, the smell of sandalwood, of yoga mats, bathroom-tile smiles, tight shirts, the sounds of —

Until they could be replaced in time, they had to stay as empty plots, weeded beds with upturned soil, not yet ready for planting.

My body hums in a pause-state, unsure where to go but taut with the need to move. I hover like the hummingbird, with a heart rate of 1200 beats per minute. (From facts the children know about animals: relative to their size, hummingbirds have the largest hearts in the animal world: 2.5% of their bodyweight is heart. The human sits at 0.3%. With my condition, I might sit at 0.5% and 72 beats pm. Hummingbirds live intensely and usually only for 3–5 years. There are none in this country.)

THE NANNY: Your body is problematic.

My body is what was fought for — its reproductive capabilities, its capacity for pleasure, its access to property, His access to it, the badge of status it conveyed. Now it must be controlled, even in defeat.

THE POET: The inability to deny access to one's own body is a state of deep powerlessness. Conversely, the ability to access everything is power. This is why you continue to feel destabilised. This why you mortify your body yet.

(I reduce in order to be free enough.)

THE ARCHER: Changing your name back might be a start. You still carry His—

For the children!

THE ARCHER: The children will be okay or not okay, regardless.

I should probably eat — my head is beginning to spin a little — but I feel overwhelmed. It was Teilhard de Chardin, the French Jesuit priest, who understood that our necessity for food is an agonising spiritual bind, with its unavoidable creation of suffering. There is anxiety in eating for me. I want to eat sunlight like plants do; anything else feels fraught. Mostly, though, my appetite has gone, churned away by worry, my stomach shredded by stress; occasionally a bone-hunger grips me, and I eat and eat as if I had suddenly awoken to life (always mostly plants).

THE ARCHER: Your refusal of all appetites is a radical escape from enclosure and entrapment.

I grow unbidden.

THE ARCHER: You are the espaliered pear tree, fruiting, with your body — your cheek — forced up against a cement wall.

THE POET: And now Emerson's earth laughs in flowers.

A dirty swell of wind curls around the corner and crashes over me — smoke and dust — and my eyes sting, roam the streets, the buses, the riots of shop windows with clothes, clothes, clothes, mismatched shoes treading the pavement, pyramids of fruit and the circular brooms of the streetsweepers, and the yelling man and the cars and the prams and the hissing steam of the coffee shops; waves of piped music crashing up against each other, the wildly perfumed candles, shining mirrors and floors and walls, the faulty fluorescent light that flickers over and over and in all of this — in all of this! — I am unable to find a pleasing order. It feels like the world is spinning too fast; the shock of details is enough to drive me mad.

Leave here now.

My body is shifting back and forth between dimensions, and I risk dislocation: here we have commercial time, moving along various parallel lines, reflected in the ordered line of shop fronts; here we have cyclical time — invisible, unpredictable, destabilising in strange ways.

I step backwards into a small sushi-train restaurant, position myself by the mini conveyor belt, and ask for a miso soup. The order will buy me time on a corner stool, and time to be left alone to stare at the little coloured plates as they make their circuit around the room.

My body is extra sensitive to everything: expressions on faces, the smell of warm vinegar rice and raw fish, the voices swelling, I feel things too clearly without thinking them, I sense more than I want to — more than I can cope with; I see too far in. I want to hide and listen to the music of Hildegarde von Bingen and burn palo santo and draw the curtains. This is not a time for sunshine smiles and the chatter of white-tiled talk that clatters and gleams hard fixed fast, stacked and ordered. This is a time for stories.

(Where is the darkness?)

I feel that my female form has so many openings into the unknown; it is fluid — it has many doors into the dark. It seeks reciprocity with the sensuous … it allows the world to touch it in many more ways.

(I am not ready to be touched.)

I watch the chefs with their knives like razors and carefully organised Tupperware: there is order here in this little sushi-train. The kitchen area is meticulous, and the plates travel on a fixed path at a fixed speed, taken and replaced at intervals but always the same, even in their variations. Watching the circuit calms me a little. It requires nothing from me; it is ordered and quiet and efficient, a self-sustaining routine with just the right degree of monotony. Safer now, I allow myself to gently redirect.

The Japanese aesthetic appreciates the power of Shadows — straight-edged structures become shoji screens where paper glows with unseen lamps and shadowy figures move, distinct but still mysterious. Here in the shadows is the possibility of linking to a vast common time, a dimension of history more like a collective sensation than a series of recorded events. It is here that is becomes possible to pass through the veil; shadows are thin places, too, where the dimness is elastic, stretching from the present back in time and forwards, all at once. The hunt for shadows is an expedition towards the Edge of Things, the forming of shapes from the purely shapeless Black that lies beyond the edges of the light-strafed world.

I remember the Balinese shadow puppets from my time in Indonesia, a wayang kulit theatre somewhere near Ubud. There, the puppeteer or dalang is a priest, a shaman, who calls in the shadows to heal and unconfuse the hearts of those who come to watch them. The shadowplay brings balance, draws out sickness, protects communities from the anger of the gods and the malevolence of demons. The dalang's role is caretaker and protector, not only of his own heart, but the heart of the village, the heart of the world.

THE POET: Move with the light, spin with wind, do not impose or assume or trample. You have a responsibility to existence to care deeply. When sunflowers are deprived of the sun — when they are kept in pure darkness — they turn and bend towards one another.

(I am bending towards you now.)

I feel I have shadow-shifted all my life — tomboy child, reluctant woman, wife, mother-to-be, mother. From one day to the next, I have become something entirely Other to what I was before. And now? Divorced single mother? My deviation from the script seems to have caused havoc.

I tried to shrink my body, to minimise it, to apologise by

taking up less and less space. I step aside, I smile, I speak very quietly. There is an existential exhaustion that bleeds around my paper edges. Some days I feel like my insistence — my persistent refusal to get out of the way or die or disappear is upsetting society's order completely.

THE ARCHER: Despite your best efforts.

Do you blame me for craving disappearance?

THE ARCHER: No.

THE NANNY: It comes down to the issue of control. That which cannot be controlled by language and legislation must be ignored or destroyed.

THE ARCHER: Ignored and destroyed. It is possible that one leads to the other or even that both happen at once.

THE POET: You appear both utterly vulnerable and utterly unknowable/unreachable. The cephalopod. It drives Them mad.

I smile into my soup and make a V-sign with my fingers like Winston Churchill. Perhaps on the lighter days that is victory enough. I imagine myself stalking an ocean floor, stepping backwards on two of my eight marvellous legs, a strategic and cunning predator, cycling through skin colours like a fairground or vanishing as sand as I lie in ambush. If we pay enough attention, there are many ways the world shows us that things are not always what they seem ... Like the atomic ash that fell on the Marshall Islands after the Castle Bravo hydrogen bomb: the children thought it was 'Bikini snow' and ate it. (When things are not as they should be ...)

(*I think of my children.*)

They say a mother's love is the symbol and true north of all the love in the universe. It is the most potent force in the world. I read about an army of women in Africa who defend elephants against poachers: they say there is no power in the world greater than that of a mother defending her children. (Here I had collapsed under the weight of this on my heart muscle. Enlarged — according to the cardiologist's ultrasounds — but not stronger. Just enlarged, oversensitive, twisting itself like a candy cane around and around the bittersweet pain.)

I love you. I long for you.

I order tea so I can sit a little longer here in my corner. I consider taking a small plate from the treadmill, but the next to pass me is a dish with tentacles, and I have to look away.

That is not an ending I can participate in.

Through the window, standing on the street outside, I see a woman I know. She is the kind of person who is powered by the news of others, taking energy from knowing more than everyone else and sharing it freely. She is not someone I wish to run into today. Now her left hand is clamped to her head as the wind tugs and tugs at the ropes of perfect ringlets that hang from it, ripping at them like a schoolyard bully. I see her head turn this way and that, her eyes check her phone, scan the crowd again, deciding whether or not to step into the restaurant and out of the wind. Fortunately, her eyes are programmed to spot shiny things — diamonds, watches, gold; hair, nails, teeth — not shadows hunched in shadows sipping an unglamorous tea. She walks on.

I am sand.

Ultimately, mine is a crisis of evolution. I have refused to change to become more suited to an environment I have no wish to belong to. I have resisted the mandate to adapt to fit a situation I did not want to find myself in, and this has caused Trouble. I stopped lying; I stopped pretending, and wallpapering over cracks, and fighting back tears over spilt milk and upset applecarts, and all the other domestic metaphors that conjured the fatal patience required to live with a dominating, controlling man. I have turned sideways into the light.

There have been rituals to negotiate. Like the gap where an invitation would have been extended but now cannot be because invitations come in pairs, as do decent humans. I find myself unable to perform the social dance required to ease the awkwardness of others. (He has already re-partnered (is that the word?) with his best friend's wife's best friend, Kendra — who is also a runner of occasional marathons, and has shiny black hair, uncomplicated and prominent abdominal muscles; no children yet — so His flow has not been interrupted. I know I never will.)

In refusing to participate in the public performance of what — sorrow? contrition? gratitude for their attention? gossip? — I have created a gap, the possibility for more truth. This is too much for most people to bear; sometimes it is too much for me to bear. The gap feels like a chasm, yawning and groaning, rumbling with hunger, and I am disorientated, afraid of what I've done. I have crossed a line; I have transgressed. This place I find myself in is not anywhere anyone wants to travel to.

Polynesian wayfinders say that to find your way in the ocean you must first see your destination in your mind's eye, and then you can never be lost. I am trying to practise this, with mixed results. I try to list navigation systems that lie outside of the GPS on my phone: the maps of sea currents made by the Polynesians who created stick charts — the earliest nautical charts — with shells and sticks; my grandfather's map of the bed of the ocean, all mountains and gullies and islands, resolved in beautiful shades of indigo — a world in reverse. It hung on his study wall in Zurich, and I made sure I was always the one sent to call him for dinner so I could get a glimpse of it. Then, most thrillingly of all, there is mycelium and the 'wood-wide web'. That is something I can pin all my faith on: the problem-solving, adaptive properties of fungi, so miraculous that in my quieter moments I imagine their intricate interweavings underpinning everything below ground and blurring the categorical edges between beings above ground. My mind stretches to try to understand the implications, and to understand why this isn't one of the most important things we know.

I cannot do this for very long before my mind begins to spin off its axis; it's like trying to count stars.

(Perhaps the only way for me to belong is to invent a universe.)

AS PART OF MY efforts to pass unnoticed — to discover what the world might be like without me in it — I experiment with moving through the world without a trace. I make myself as small, energetically and physically, as possible. I eat less, I become Less. I slide through turnstiles, avoid touching railings, duck into doorways, slip through closing doors with my hands in my pockets; I wear oversized clothes that shrink me. I stop speaking. I strive to become a blade, to sharpen, to feel the fiercer edges of experience, to take up less room. I turn side-on into the sun and vanish, my shadow the lamppost, the traffic pole, the pen. I excuse myself with silence from the conversations I no longer wish to have. My hiding is active, conscious; I long to un-belong.

This hiding is an attempt to reach around the back of this monstrous electronic edifice we have created and to pull out the plug. It hints at the promising future emergence of a different state of being...

When everything is spoken for — named and tamed — I will un-name it. What if there emerged a new grammar, verbs made from nouns, new understandings created by the unlocking of manacled phrases? What if categories between Things collapsed — human, non-human, material — and the wild things were set free and what if the inclusions of this new transmission were so bountiful that they overflowed and could not be contained by the forces who wish to house for themselves the power that comes with the control of importance and implication and consequence and value and worth ...

THE ARCHER: What then?

'In the beginning was the word and the word was God.'

(They have known from the start the power of that and claimed language as Theirs.)

There is elegance in refusal, in disentangling from the entanglements of others, in resisting the pull — the rip-tide — of the narrative arc they have written for you. The story will always be too small; you will be miscast if cast at all. You will perpetually be a bit player in their story; you will never be cast in the main role, not even as the Love Interest. You will be: BRUNETTE, THREE ROWS BACK. (Not a speaking part).

I make my way to a cinema within walking distance of the sushi train, trembling. I crave the relief of momentarily making myself vanish — absenting myself temporally from Being in that day, erasing any identity by sitting in silence in the dark. The choice feels bold and disorientating and like an expression of freedom all at once. Agnes Varda's statement on the poster promoting her film *Le Bonheur* draws me in: **If we opened people up, we'd find landscapes** (yes) — and I buy a single ticket, a single carton of popcorn, and a lemonade. The cool, dark cinema is the deepest relief after the hot streets outside. I choose a seat five rows back and slightly to the right of the screen. There are three other women in the theatre, planted apart like saplings, also alone.

I know instantly and instinctively what has bought them to a French film on a Wednesday afternoon: they are practising. They are practising living outside of their daily lives, trying to feel what it would be like to be unreachable, to belong to themselves again. It gives us all an air of quivering audacity, of terrified recklessness that charges the theatre before the film has even begun. We sit with our single popcorn cartons in perfect silence, eyes fixed ahead, faces pale in the low light, waiting for the curtains to part.

There is no solidarity in this moment. We are all guilty; none of us is seeking complicity with each other. We are all there to forget, to be forgotten, to forget ourselves for an hour; to inhabit bodies and worlds more vivid than the one outside, to wake in bed to a tousled Frenchman, a cigarette, a moving soundtrack, and into a life of Possibilities and the Eventual Revelation of an order we suspect is dangerously lacking in our own.

We have lost our faith in the future as a safe place for our dreams, a sunlit repository, a stretching place where Things Could Still Be. We are no longer confident in the choices we have made. We spin possibilities — indecisions, visions and revisions — paths re-trodden, those left untaken, those doubling back to loop on themselves, those that lead to a sinkhole in the earth. We have taken the wrong train and now find ourselves lost, the map of coloured lines, names, unintelligible to us, now wondering where to change, where to get off the train, how to get off the train ...

THE POET: You left because you had chosen the wrong future.

Time as Train, as Straight Arrow forced upon the circular situations of organic life ... No one in the theatre is young. We have all lived enough to — to get to this point in our lives. The desire for erasure permeates the velvet air: could I do it? Do I dare?

Do I dare?

The echoes of J. Alfred Prufrock grow loud now —

Do I dare to eat a peach?

... think of all those coffee spoons ...

... I should begin rolling my trouser hems ...

... that yellow smog ...

In the same way children will make a cubby in the living room with a blanket and two chairs to watch the secret life of adults unfold without them — to practise living alone — so we few had come to the cinema during the day. We are rehearsing for a future disappearance.

Like young children who close their eyes and believe no one can see them.

Like middle-aged women, our jeans rolled softly to rest on the slenderest part of the ankle, tired now — so tired — of preparing our faces to greet all those rooms.

(I close my eyes; I have no faces left in me.)

I pick up a single kernel of popcorn with my tongue, summoning the focus required to do this in an effort to still the interrupting voices.

THE NANNY: Please focus on the film. Agnes Varda will shift your lens.

The children come this evening.

THE NANNY: But you are at the cinema now. Focus on the moment. The anticipation could be dangerous. He might change his mind.

I banish that thought like a baseball batter swinging to hit the ball out of the park, and with as much violence.

The anticipation is how I hold them when we are apart. It's how I can love them when they are not here.

THE ARCHER: You could see the separation as practice for when they grow up and leave you.

The red velvet curtain draws slowly back, the lights dim further, the tears roll.

I am not ready.

THE NANNY: The children come this evening. Don't forget to buy the milk.

DURING OUR SEPARATION, WE had been required to see a marriage therapist. Her name was Magdalena — from Chile — and she had sat in her small room with the mohair rug and the plants and the books on Jung and talked about gardens. She had explained that marriage was a shared garden: you had your individual garden beds and then another one in the middle, surrounded by a wall and two doors, and you could enter separately to spend time there. The idea of a walled garden had enchanted me — an old apple tree, a bench, roses, wild grasses.

He was more of a 'collective agriculture' Soviet Kolkhoz type of farmer: the plants are enslaved and have forgotten how to communicate with each other; walls are not good if they protect the rights of Others; everything is One. His One. By the end of the session, the metaphor had shattered: my raging mood disorder — my lunacy! — was front and centre of the session, my selfishness, my failure to discipline the children properly.

'They need contact,' He had repeated. 'They won't listen without contact!'

'Use your words,' I automatically responded in my head.

I stopped speaking. There was no room for me. The therapist met my eyes and held them a while. She saw more than she could say.

'I think we lost Winona somewhere along the —'

He interrupted her before she could help me.

In the end, it was almost two hours of talking. Him talking.

At least Magdalena had experienced the Waterfall Effect for herself. It was easier than having to explain with — more words. We left separately, Him first. When I judged enough time had passed for Him to have safely left the building, I got up to go. Magdalena took my hand as if to shake it, and then held it for long enough for me to understand she was telegraphing a message that was perhaps unprofessional, perhaps unsafe — very likely both — to speak aloud: 'I am trying to help you find an alternative, a space in the world where two diametrically opposed ideas of Living can be fought over within boundaries. Boundaries offer the possibility of a truce, a peace, however uneasy; without the safely of these, there is only the annihilation of One. It is not always possible to avoid conflict, but there must exist the option of withdrawal or else what is there?'

I replied in kind, liberated to speak honestly to her at last, even if it was just with my eyes.

I am trying to withdraw from this war with an enemy that I never wanted but to whom I find myself inextricably bound. He has badly wounded me and has plans to do so again and again. How can any peace be found in a situation like this that does not call for total capitulation?

'I must speak frankly and secretly: He has encouraged in you day after day a desperate hope that you can make peace and restore order and rescue your children from distress.'

He is lying to me?

'No, He is allowing you to lie to yourself. He doesn't need to deceive you. He only needs to feed with small hopes your desperation for Things to Be Better Than They Are.'

That is a different sort of deception, running not against Truth but against Life. How can I escape from that?

'It may never leave you.'

We vibrated a moment together in understanding and silence in that little room in a crumbly building, with its alpaca cushions and smell of furniture polish. I understood why Magdalena needed so many plants — so many Frequency Holders and Emanators — in her room.

I thanked her and turned to leave. I found myself in a small falling spiral — disorientated by the undeniable truth of what she had conveyed — but I appreciated her honesty. It meant I had poked out of my skin enough to touch her; I had been heard, or rather, my silencing had been witnessed. Magdalena did not think I was crazy.

She said as much to me over the phone later, in careful words: *I don't see any indications ...* although even she had had the good sense not to say this in the Shared Garden.

When I told Him that Magdalena did not think I was mentally ill, He decided we had to find another therapist who was more sensible. A man. A local. A friend of a friend.

Almost there.

The whole thing was a series of Almost There's, and in that lay the deadly edge. The Impossible can be flirted with as a fantasy that sometimes tips over into the realm of the possible, but the Almost There ... that something so within reach that the sinews and tendons of the arm ache and stretch, and you almost have the satisfaction of having it, so close, close enough to feel that every struggle that has come before was worth it. Then you realise that between your fingertips and your goal — those missing three centimetres separating you from Everything — is a thick sheet of glass, soundproof and bulletproof glass, in fact. And shout as you might, or bang or scratch, on the other side of the glass, no one hears you and nothing changes. The death of hope then is so much more painful for having come so close. The stakes could not have been higher, and the glass could not have been thicker.

And a moment has come and gone — that curious instant when the world as you believe it to be comes undone before you, when your deepest beliefs are shaken — when a new idea offers you a lungful of a different reality and you are giddy with the oxygen of it. I had spent years looking in the wrong direction, and now I was being forced to stare at something I should always have seen.

The whys, hows, and wheres belong to a story told by Lawyers and The People Who Keep Notes. This story matters, but I can't summon the strength to glance back there. For this you will have to trust me, trust the words of a woman who is mad, who cannot be controlled, a deviant.

I have not recorded the screaming, the crashing, the slamming. The sound of eggshells cracking as we tiptoe doesn't register on a microphone. Silence can mean peace and also death. In our case, silence is an imperative. No one is allowed to say what happened. Because I didn't just sail off into the sunset one windy evening with the kids and live happily ever after. There was an intention and a vision, then there was the reality.

It turns out the historians are right: no one ever cedes power; it has to be taken.

No one sailed off into the sunset because He refused to leave the house. That was not something He was prepared to do. I'd bought the place with my grandmother's legacy, and it had become valuable. There was too much money at stake for

Him, and the optics would be poor. For two years, we lived with Him there. I moved myself into the little study. It had one small window, and was lined on three walls with books from floor to ceiling. It was the safest room in the house, with a low daybed that became my bed. The children refused to sleep in theirs and made nests on either side of me with their mattresses, and sheepskins, and duvets. We were three souls together in this strange torn nest, ears pricked for footfalls. He stayed in the master bedroom with the en-suite and the walk-in robe. We stayed as quiet as mice as He passed our sliding doors. There was no lock, and we felt this keenly.

We found ourselves living in a world within a world: a heterotopia ruled by laws that inverted the ordinary, rules that were unique, immersive, invisible — even unknowable — to anyone on the outside. It was also not a space that anyone outside our family could enter. (Other examples of heterotopias are: pirate ships, brothels, cemeteries; boarding schools, asylums, and prisons.)

A MENU OF IMPRESSIONS:

He roamed the house in His underpants, stretching and whistling. It was completely unnverving. As intended. I had to use the kitchen to make breakfasts and pack lunches; I would wait until I heard the shower. The footsteps and the whistling, a strange circus-clown cheeriness that freaked us the fk out. There was, most days, some explosion at the moment it was time to get to school. I would intervene with my best 'conflict resolution' skills, which I've studied from a therapy booklet. Sometimes I'd feel that I'd succeeded and would feel capable and strong. Then my boy told me that on those days, He waited for them to be locked in the car and then screamed all the way to school; I stopped trying to resolve conflicts and instead did every drop-off and pick-up myself. It was like trying to bail a tanker with a coffee cup.

The weekends were the worst, as He rarely left the house. There could have been no more exquisite domestic torture for me. I clung to the outside edges, hugged the walls, circled in stocking feet. My antennae were in high-receive the entire time, trying to detect any subsonic rumblings that could develop into something a lot more. I couldn't leave the house without the children and there were only so many parks we could visit.

Most weeknights, He'd go out to see people and we would have a reprieve. We'd have to get into our safe room before He got home. The sound of the door from the garage clicking open triggered some kind of Pavlovian response. We all visibly flinched. My dreams made sure there was no rest. I craved the oblivion of sleep without a diorama of distress — to forget — but would wake in the morning in the library, surrounded by the jumble of limbs, hear a toothbrush tap in a sink along the corridor and feel sick all over again. I lost eight kilos and my ability to focus for more than three, four minutes. I started at noises and woke sweating from nightmares. I wanted to cry all the time.

We had to sell the house so He could get half the money, the money He felt He was entitled to, and move out. It was hard to do — I am certain the strange atmosphere could be felt. Every time the realtor came, I had to drag the children's 'beds' to their rooms and transform the study back into a room for books. To make it look as if normal lives were being lived there. It was exhausting and felt Sisyphean. I erased our traces over and over again. (I still bought His food. I felt somehow that it would be a dangerous line to cross, to stop buying the ingredients for His breakfast protein smoothies. That would have broken the fourth wall in the play that had become our life.)

I consulted Maslow's Hierarchy of Needs; I created my own compendium:

<u>WINONA'S GLOSSARY OF THREATS:</u>
by Winona Dalloway
- (I never completed this list)

There were days when I tore at myself with frustration and rage and helplessness. I wanted to run and run and run. But there was nowhere I could go, and I had no way to buy another house. I trembled so hard I couldn't hold a pen; my bowels were water.

We lived like that for two years.

I STILL ENTERTAIN COOL and limpid fantasies of vanishment, of escape to the other side of the world, of an Act of God that will stack the deck suddenly and irreversibly in my favour. No act has come so far; my vanishment is something I must play out on my own in the small ways that I have found to do so— myriad micro-expressions of a freedom I survived for so long without.

I have my own space now — my rented bungalow — but my children are being withheld from me; the attempts to control me have merely evolved. He will not pay alimony, He will not pay child support. I refuse to battle this; I know in my bones it would become another lever of control for Him. I am determined to make it work on my own; it is imperative to be wholly independent of Him — it is a crucial part of How to Appear to Disappear.

<u>HOW TO APPEAR TO DISAPPEAR</u>
by Winona Dalloway
- Do not engage in any battles that are not crucial to your survival
- Become incredibly boring: no one wants to talk about you or to you
- Do not react emotionally to any communication (see previous)
- Become physically small; hide your face in hoodies and behind sunglasses

- Demand nothing; be silent
- Walk into a river like Virginia Woolf, a lake like Varda's Thérèse, the sea like Ann Quin — so many bodies of water, one ultimate erasure

(SUB-LIST OF SAFE ACTIVITIES AND PLACES)
- supermarkets
- remote cliff tops and bushland
- the sea (surface)
- buses and trains
- libraries
- bookstores

Attending a matinee at the cinema is also on the list. Varda's *Le Bonheur* — *Happiness* — is a terrifying movie. Does that make it unsafe or the safest thing of all?

THE ARCHER: Thérèse was interchangeable too, Winona.

THE CHILD: There were sunflowers!

THE NANNY: It's a horror story —

THE POET: A beautiful horror film about love and happiness set to Mozart.

It's the first film I have since watched about love that has made any sense.

THE NANNY: You know you cannot disappear. This is not an option for you. You must find alternative ways to appear.

(*Yes.*)

Yes. Disappearance is the refuge of the powerless and it is not enough. There will be no bolt of lightning, no dragon, no white horse in this city that does not allow animals to appear in un-designated spaces, in this city with a reputation for being easy-going but where the population lives with its nose pressed up against the glass.

THE CHILD: Winona, you are the poinsettia, and you must rescue yourself.

THE ARCHER: NO ONE IS COMING FOR YOU, WINONA. THIS IS NOT A HOLLYWOOD FILM.

(This is not a Hollywood film. This is the realest thing that has happened to me since childbirth.)

I have flailed around inside — fish on hook — trying to find the narrative that will lead me out of my wilderness, but I come up short. I am safe neither inside nor outside the marriage; I do not feel safe anywhere. Madness is a dangerous label for any woman to wear — for some, it might even be lethal. In 1792, during the French Revolution, mobs opened the gates of the all-female Salpêtrière Hospital for the indigent and the insane in Paris. When the women fled their prison, thirty-five of them were raped and bludgeoned to death by the waiting crowds.

When my boy refused to leave me, and threw himself down a flight of stone steps, I refused to force him further. His lawyers said the incident was my fault — my instability provokes it in my son; my madness is contagious. He will remove the children by the force of The Law. The terror of this. Everyone knows what happens when the Law gets involved. A court would turn from our distress and listen only to the stories of my lunacy. He has so many documents and papers and reports — I wish I wish I wish I had known what to do. (And I still don't know.) I wish I had not trusted that the good would be seen and the children protected because surely, surely — my naivety was breathtaking, and I had not forgotten this lesson. I had no faith in a system that couldn't protect us.

They made them go.

THE ARCHER: They made you complicit in this.

(*I will never forgive myself.*)

THE ARCHER: You must take responsibility — blame even — but you must also rise. Anyone who rises after falling, or having been tripped, is threatening — a troublemaker, impossible to control, deviant, dangerous.

Yes.

THE POET: Remember that nature's cycle is a devouring one, it is not gentleness: the talon of the hawk, the dead shark, the crushing power of glaciers, the near-death of the surfer ...

THE NANNY: Playing Dead is a strategy of animals in the wild.

THE CHILD: So is camouflage.

THE ARCHER: And poison.

THE POET: Oak trees create salic acid in their leaves when their brethren upstream get a plague of caterpillars. So, too, mysteriously move the currents of knowledge, and our invisible defences marshal.

THE CHILD: Be the plant.

THE ARCHER: That's a little passive!

THE CHILD: The ceding parry was always your favourite fencing move.

THE NANNY: This is a good point.

THE POET: Play to your strengths. Do not provoke the Narcissistic Rage — isn't that what they say? Run. If you can't run, then hide. Play the long game. Resist. Learn from the Maquis.

And so I do.

THE NANNY: And so you do.

THE ARCHER: And what of the children?

(*Silence here, too, is an imperative.*)

THE NANNY: This is a weapon he can only use once.

He has used it. And it is done. He has done his worst. I am still here.

'My life had stood — a loaded gun.' (Emily Dickinson)

THE ARCHER: Becoming visible to the police is not on the List of How to Appear to Disappear.

(*No. That belongs on a different list altogether.*)

THE FIRST TIME THE police came was in the middle of a weekday. The three of us had moved into the new place by then, and the boys were at school. Picture the scene, if you will:

INT. SUBURBAN HOME — KITCHEN — DAY

WINONA is unloading a dishwasher.

O.S DOORBELL

WINONA jumps, startled, and moves tentatively to the front door. She looks through the SPYHOLE

POV WINONA

DISTORTED BY LENS

TWO POLICEMEN in uniform stand at the front door (POLICEMAN 1 is tall and blond; POLICEMAN 2 smaller and dark-haired). The LENS makes their guns and tasers and eyes appear huge.

INT. KITCHEN — DAY

Winona opens the door. Over her shoulder we see the faces of the two policemen.

                POLICEMAN 1
        (Indistinct; voice distorted)

                  WINONA
    Yes, of course.

They entered. I had never been visited by the police before, and this was unlikely to be good. I was glad I had mostly tidied the house. They didn't want a glass of water nor to sit down. We hovered awkwardly in my little kitchen. They wore heavy black boots and took up far more room inside the house than they did on my doorstep. I moved behind the kitchen bench to put a barrier between us, to be closer to my plantlings, whom I could almost feel quivering with uncertainty at the arrival of these new beings in our home.

The station had received a phone call reporting someone breaking into a ground-floor flat in my street — a caretaker's flat. Although the flat was empty, it was still a break-in, and they had to follow up. The caller apparently recognised me from my walks around the neighbourhood, saw me take something from the flat, knew where I lived. For a moment, I considered complete denial, but I knew I was unlikely to pull it off and anyway, the liberated poinsettia was practically cheering its red petal pom-poms in greeting from the bench.

You know, it's a funny story ...

I imagined explaining the Vision: that circles of compassion can begin with plants and widen, that the liberation of plants is a powerful flanking move. People don't care about plants as they do puppies. No one leaves puppies out to die on the road, and if they do, everyone agrees it is cruel, outrageous, immoral, and unconscionable.

Begin with plants and expand. Liberate the world from its carapace of uncaring! This can feel a little overwhelming as an idea to contemplate properly, I do agree, like counting stars or listening to someone tell you that the entire universe was a reverse-projection of the inside of our minds ... but it can be done!

I settled instead for: I was walking past. I thought I heard a cry of distress (true; the plant). The flat looked abandoned, and I called out and pushed the door. It was open (I decided it was best to omit mentioning the bower bird, the key, the conflagrations of fate that led to my noticing the door). I entered, called out, saw nothing amiss except a plant dying on the windowsill.

(I took the plant.)

I pointed to the poinsettia on the bench who is smiling blithely, unaware of what is at stake here. (I wondered briefly whether the cacti, or even the monstera, would have been a little more reticent — discrete — in their emanations in the face of Authoritative Law Enforcement Vibrations, weapons, bulletproof vests.) My face was burning; my hands were visibly and uncontrollably shaking.

The taller of the men took notes; the smaller of the two policemen stared at my hands. He lifted his gaze to my face and gave me That Look. I recognised it before I could put the word-encasement around the Knowing that formed the Thought.

Dismay and terror; heat and nausea flushed upwards through my body. My throat fought back despair, caught between the windpipe and the oesophagus.

Fire!

THE NANNY: No. You can't lose it here, Win. Ignore the look. Prove him wrong. Cast Doubt and Aspersions on the information he has obviously been told.

But why does he think those things?? He doesn't know me. He has never met me! Why is he looking at me with that mix, so familiar, of distaste, contempt, fear, and condescension all jumbled together? It can't just be the plant. Micro-expressions he cannot control, and which I can read Loud and Clear. It's not a look one happens upon casually, gives accidentally —

THE ARCHER: It's the look that says, 'Crazy lady — I know about you.'

(beat)

THE ARCHER: Why do you think, Win?

No!

(Silence.)

(*No.*)

THE NANNY: Think about the only reason that makes any sense here. I'll let you take your time, but it can't be forever. Smaller Man is waiting for you to speak more. Your delay is not helping your situation.

Tears of frustration, of fear, of confusion were gathering their forces but I could not permit them free reign. I swallowed the lump in my throat and exhaled. It was as if my very spirit were being forced out of my body.

'I'm so sorry. I really don't know what came over me. I can return the plant if that ...'

That was not what they were interested in. The smaller man wandered proprietorially about my kitchen, a Gargamel amongst my plant Smurfs. His huge rubber-soled shoes made no sound. He peered at my pinboard, my fridge, the rows of shoes lined up neatly in the hall, the recycling stacked by the door ... Then back at me. It was the taller one who broke the silence: they would issue me with a warning. It is against the law to break into houses even if they are empty; it is not permitted to remove objects from the premises. It would go into a report.

The smaller one turned to me and asked: 'Sooo ...' — that vowel-drag, the telegraphing of something unpleasant—'howseverythingathome?'

He ran his words together like a freight train so weighted with suspicion that they sank into me and fell right through. I let them fall, and it was only a beat later that I understood them and things became clear.

I stare at him.

'Fine, thanks.'

He turned to his own notebook, making a show of flipping through pages, even though he already knew exactly what he was going to say:

'We've had reports made about your behaviour previous to this incident.'

THE POET: (And her blossoms go up like dust.)

He had rung the station on several occasions to report His concern about my behaviour. Apparently, there is now a record of me that I hadn't known existed: allegations of erratic behaviour, child endangerment, unco-operative behaviour, disruptive behaviour.

'When He came to collect the children, you screamed at Him and He felt threatened and intimidated ...'

(more notebook flipping)

'You threw half a hamburger and a paper cup of strawberry smoothie at His car as he drove away.'

'But I don't eat meat ...'

Another Look told me this was clearly not the right thing to say.

'He reports that you regularly call at all hours of the night to shout at Him, and you have been spotted standing outside His bedroom window — also at night — on more than one occasion.'

I couldn't imagine doing a single one of these things. Surely I would have remembered hurling a milkshake? I was so bewildered by the size of the untruth that I was disorientated and then it became clear, clear, clear as day —

clear smear near fear leer dear; seer freer rear hear sheer beer buccaneer commandeer bombardier tier spear ear

THE NANNY: What you have here, Winona, is a Firehose of Falsehoods.

(Yes.)

The Firehose of Falsehoods is a propaganda technique used effectively by the contemporary Russian state: rather than contradict or counter facts with partial truths or careful distortions, they simply overwhelm and confuse any notions of the truth with mass disinformation. This strategy is characterised by a high and various number of channels used —

THE NANNY: In your case: doctors, psychiatrists, school principals, other parents, the police, as well as more generalised gossip, and the shameless broadcasting of complete fictions.

While the effect on the police, and any subsequent reports if you end up in the Family Court, obviously has the potential to be problematic for you, this is about more than simple lies. A Firehose of Falsehoods is not primarily employed to make you doubt your own memory, even to convince you — it is an expression of power designed to make you afraid. The more extreme or ridiculous the spray of lies, the more potent it is. Power is inversely proportionate to Truth, because the only person who can tell a wholly unbelievable lie is one with an utterly inviolable sense of their own power to control events, to control you. The wild lie says, 'Of course you don't believe this, but I am so unassailable in my dominance that I don't need you to believe it.'

THE POET: The greater the lie, the more profound and total the expression of power.

Fragments of Small's sentences broke into my thoughts —

'... instances of intimidation ... following up any future complaints ...'

Lunacy — a dangerous lunacy — had been more than inferred: it had been outright declared, down to strange and particular details like the flavour of the milkshake. The fact that it was unsubstantiated and untrue did little to counter the fact that a police record existed.

'We will be keeping an eye on you.'

I nodded.

(It would be better if you were keeping a) both eyes open and b) focused where they should be.)

I pushed away the chill that accompanied the Sudden Knowing that He had been seeding my insanity with the police, with his lawyers, doctors — others — for months. I was a problem to be dispensed with, and here were a series of violent shoves towards self-slaughter. At that point, something inside me turned to water — I almost wanted to give up.

THE POET: And these, then, are the structures of a new tyranny ...

THE ARCHER: A cairn of sharp stones has been carefully gathered —

THE CHILD: You must build your own cairn!

THE POET: You must set your story against his. This is a matter of (your) life and death. This formal language of authority masks then distorts its true purpose; structural violence — any violence — will always be a playing field in which He and others like Him dominate. To resist, you can only refuse to engage on their terms; flit and dash between the bars of this structure, set a bomb against the steel door, bake a file into the birthday cake. You must unpick the single narrative, confuse its strands, explode its organising principle and make a kaleidoscope from the pieces. There will be no way to put the pieces back as they were.

THE NANNY: Story fast becomes legend with the telling, neatly dotted now with the markers of the hero's journey, let loose from the space it occupies in place and time into something vast. You must act before you are miscast as Ophelia, as Medusa ...

THE ARCHER: This is a vexed hierarchy.

THE CHILD: Blow it up!

I find it soothing to watch explosions in reverse, where everything is coming back together: a retreat into wholeness. The implosion of fireworks is particularly satisfying.

There will be no acknowledgement of what is being fought for here in my small world. It will be like the plane that tumbles into the sea: no evidence that it ever happened. The waters close over. There are no witnesses who can speak; it is enough to drive anyone mad.

He has turned the community with dark talk of my contagion ... I don't need to know what He says; I see the consequences in the way They look at me, light bending Their glances to suspicious squints and worse. In fact, it is most awful of all when They seek me out with false concern, Their eyes raking me over and over, probing, taking, storing information for future rumours. The dark matter has bent the fabric of spacetime, and now I stand alone. The nursery rhyme repeats 'the cheese stands alone, the cheese stands alone, hi ho the dairy-o the cheese stands alone.'

cone bone hone sewn loan drone roan zone moan crone atone

It is important that I be expelled from social networks — detached, removed, shunned, undermined. It is both painful and confusing; I feel the Eyes everywhere I go, and they are not kind eyes.

Take that man — similar age to Him, similar hair and clothing — who spotted me having an early dinner out with my sons. We had just moved into our new home; I was feeling free and hopeful, and we had decided on a spontaneous plate of pasta to celebrate. The man approached our table and greeted me by name, stared too intently at me. I had no idea who he was, but I smiled at him politely, kindly even, unguarded, guessing I had likely forgotten our first meeting ... He actually craned his head to look closer: 'How aaaaaaare youuu?' (the stretched vowels again!) morbid, mocking, rapaciously curious. I chilled and kept smiling as I felt my stomach turn to stone. (Repeat this or a version of this over and over and over.)

And yet, and yet, I still don't feel it is the punishment He has hoped it would be. Communion with like beings can be found outside the self-congratulatory social structures of comfortably monied suburbia. In fact, the contemplation of these structures makes me ill. I don't resist my exclusion because deep down I *want* to be rid of them, to eject myself from the echo chamber of part malicious gossip and part self-congratulation — the false humility and ersatz compassion. I tell myself it is a choice. I would rather strive alone, and keen on cliffs, and retreat into my internal wonderland. I do not want to perform my grief; I honour it for the sake of what the children have been through. More I cannot do. I would have fled as far as Greenland if I could, but two Dear Hearts mean I can only stay and try not to feel like a prisoner.

My loneliness is a well of inky sorrow that I assuage amongst non-humans. I am attempting to nurture a Lifeworld —

THE NANNY: You are in the process of rebuilding from the position of a person who does not exist anymore.

THE POET: They seek to eliminate the sources of your strength and power ... identify them, guard them, grow them.

Yes. The power of the Lifeworld lies at the heart of this: a life shared in common with others, with nature, where we can live beyond the merely instrumental and functional possibilities of a social or natural environment. Is it possible to imagine radically different ways of living and working with others and for it to not result in yet another Improving Social Experiment that ends in mass starvation, terror, and murder? (Many men have tried, and it has ended so; their experiments have many names, most are more than familiar to you.)

Winona — and here I take myself firmly in hand, for the

Agnes Varda film has finished. The credits are rolling and practical matters like finding a rubbish bin for the empty popcorn carton must be attended to.

THE NANNY: WINONA!

The wind hits me as I push open the heavy glass doors of the cinema. It is hot and smells of smoke and burning, and rasps through the street, dragging dead leaves. The doors swing back unexpectedly, shoved by the wind. I regain my balance, shoulder the door more firmly, remove strands of hair from my mouth, my eyes. There are not many people about, fewer cars even; people are staying indoors if they can. An orange kite has impaled itself on a dying bush beside the road.

I walk on.

THE POET: Expand your attention and you can expand your world ... make and shape your Lifeworld ... resist hijack by systems that force and shape our worldmaking ... seek encounters with other perceivers (Bowerbird, Poinsettia, Dog, Cockatoo, Fig) ... swell your Umwelt and assuage the species loneliness that runs like measles through your suburbs; transcend the Copernican world view that the rational intellect holds itself apart from the experiencing body.

THE NANNY: You have to give yourself away before you can regain any semblance of innocence, before you can hope to become even almost whole again.

Back at home, I begin to assemble a picnic dinner: I have two large African baskets to fill, and I remind myself to include something for Bruce should he turn up. He does have a lovely habit of appearing when I need him most.

PICNIC LIST

by Winona Dalloway
- baby carrots
- gem lettuce (lemon sauce in a jar)
- green olives
- rice crackers
- hard-boiled eggs
- two pizzas (made the evening before)
- pistachio nuts
- dried mango
- apples
- three small chocolate bears
- an orange cake (also baked the night before — I stress-cook).
- small cubes of cheese (mainly for Bruce: he is very partial to cheese).

The picnic is the best way I can think of to create Normal for us. I am an avid picnicker, and the boys and I have picnicked everywhere from car boots to mountainsides too steep to eat much more than a bread roll or an egg. We have picnicked on fishing boats in the open ocean, in botanical gardens, on beaches, and once memorably behind a waterfall. I can pretend it is a Fun Choice.

I pack and re-pack the baskets, add napkins, a knife (not too big or sharp lest that be seen as Endangeringly Violent in some way). The food is healthy — is chocolate okay or will it count against me? — the knife is blunt; the chocolate is okay; the knife is small — the list turns over and over in my head as I look for the pitfalls. I think the picnic will do. I have shopped from the

Children's List and their favourite things are here.

Shopping for myself is still disorientating: I buy the food the children like, only to throw it away when it goes bad. I am learning to catch myself.

THE NANNY: It's the little one who likes bananas, remember? You don't really like bananas. He is not at home. You don't need to buy bananas.

Bananas become, for that morning, the Fruit of Sorrow and Loss.

THE NANNY: (Bananas are blue when they're viewed under ultraviolet light; change the field of your perception, Winona.)

THE POET: Longing is a form of loving. It is a yearning, a deep bittersweet lean into a place of home and wholeness and perfection that we sense and can only catch glimpses of.

THE CHILD: Don't forget a picnic blanket: the grass is itchy!

Small actions mightily undertaken; here are some.

By the stove in my kitchen, I have a collection of small gestures — a shrine of sorts — some shells, other found objects: the empty seashell holds within it the shape of the force that formed it. Pearls and irritations, beauty from the unlikely consequences of stressors: diamonds from coal, pearls from parasites, valleys from ice, beaches from crashing water. I put small pieces of Found Blue in a nod to the bowerbird, a seedpod shaped like an angry hairy man, a shadow puppet I made of a dancing woman, a few striated stones, a candle with a brass corona of stars, an evil eye made of glass. I take long walks; I take pride in my script work as a means of independent being that bothers no one; I rescue plants and make spicy vegetable curries; I beam constant love to my boys. I take a lot of naps.

I make sure to attend to my appearance when I am to see the boys — some eyeliner and mascara, brushed hair, pearls, earrings. I try to make myself a little pretty for them, so they don't have to feel embarrassed by me. (I know what has been said in the playground, words that can only have trickled down from parents. My boy got into a fight defending me. This, of all things, broke me most.) I always wear the same perfume, so the boys remember me; I buy too much food: even the olives are gargantuan, a testament to my longing.

(Here again then we have a falling baseline syndrome: in our docility and our conformity, we undo the likelihood of remembering other ways of being, older ways, completely different ways.)

In my mind, my married life had a soundtrack; it's the best way I can describe how living it felt to me.

<u>WIFE AS A SOUNDSCAPE:</u>
By Winona Dalloway
Exercise:
You have to listen with headphones and for several days at least: you will hear humming, mostly on a low frequency with no gaps or silences, almost subsonic, soporific. You may notice sensations of unease and mild distress in your chest and stomach, a seizing of the throat. Periodically, and without warning, you will hear hard sharp riffs, cymbals, drums, a trumpet too close and loud — tight bugle, shrill, demanding electrostatic. And at random intervals, canned laughter breaking like crates of glass, breaking over everything. As the hours pass, you may begin feeling completely overwhelmed

and yet desperately underwhelmed all at once, all of it throbbing along on a bassline of —

The Leaving had a series of false starts or rather, a series of small experiments and revelations that led to greater and irreversible ones. I had been out walking, talking on the phone to a Jamaican friend, a musician who now lived with his elfin wife outside London. He told me a story about how their studio had almost burned down during a party; when he asked about my life I began to try and say something true, but I found myself struggling to make sentences. During one of my contorted pauses, he asked the tender question that broke me open: *Whata got you so man down?? Whata gwaan?*

I gasped, as if I had been hit, and I started to weep — I mean really weep, not cute crying or small, cinematic, bittersweet tears, but the kind with snot and heaving and slitty eyes and snorting; the kind that makes people stare at you. He waited on the other end of the line, not saying anything, just holding the space for me to fall apart. I sat on a bench and cradled my head in my hands, my wrists and forearms slick with tears and mucus.

Yah, irie, is what he said — *it's okay* — *yah, irie,* softly, over and over, weaving me a lifeline.

I think that was the first time I really stopped lying to myself, because I began, with thrilling audacity, to imagine myself outside my marriage. Once I started, it became impossible to reimagine my way back in: I folded the laundry — sorting tea towels and pairing socks — with free and lively fingers; I cut the crusts off school sandwiches with the Jaunty Blade of Liberty, scoured the bathtub with rubber gloves and the Elbow-grease of Emancipation. When I stopped dreaming, I began to sing.

THE POET: You sing what you cannot say.

Swing low sweet chariot ... a band of angels coming after me, coming for to carry me home.

Home is the place you no longer dream of running from.

Another friend — a New Yorker who makes strange and beautiful horror films — told me that to make a difficult decision, you have to pretend you have already made a choice and then walk a New York City block as if you had acted on that choice. Note how it feels: this will reveal what your heart truly wants to do.

I left my house barefoot one morning and walked the equivalent of a New York city block on a deserted suburban street, dodging the sticky splatters of Moreton Bay figs, the sharp stab of loose gumnuts underfoot. I walked faster and faster and faster, then I started running. I had no idea where I was going but I just knew my body — my entire being — needed to run. Maybe forever.

BRUCE: And you are not much of a runner, if I may say. (This is what he said when I explained my friend's strategy.)

'You may. And it's true. But I ran for what seemed like hours, like I was running from and towards things at once; I ran like I was possessed. I kept running for months and months, away from the terrible clarity in my heart; I ran the breadth of Antarctica, the length of Latin America, and still never found the doubt I was looking for.'

BRUCE: You are still trying to get away.

'When we walked out of the house that night, I thought it was finally over, but it had only just begun. I am still trying to get away. Since when have I become so fearful, Bruce?'

BRUCE: You know you have survived when you can start to take risks again, when you can play.

'Taking the plant was a risk.'

BRUCE: So you are on the right track. Walk on.

Every time I hear something untrue about myself, I try to add to a List of Things I Know to Be True: things I like, things I feel, the person I want to be, the people and beings I love. I add a new stone to my own cairn. It is a defence against eradication and a bulwark against the forces of All Separations.

Separateness and its Attendant Forces — divorces, lawyers, medical diagnoses, the removal of children — is in battle with the universe's longing for mutual flourishing, connectedness, and kindness. The alternative paradigm in times of chaos is a pull to truth, beauty, and goodness.

Love is the ultimate holotropic attractor.

In an effort to harness the power of these holotropic energies, I send messages to the universe, asking the boys how the maths test went, if they have eaten lunch — holding to the ephemera as if to draw them to me. Anything new that happens to them when they are not with me is a tiny needleprick of fear; I add to my list of things I love and know to be true to feel less afraid.

LIST OF THINGS I KNOW TO BE TRUE:
(subtitle: How to Rebuild a Person from Nothing)

- I like trees: trees feel pain and have a sense of taste and smell. They are social beings — they communicate — and will feed a stump among them to keep it alive. A tree alone cannot establish a microclimate: it is at the mercy of the wind and the weather; a forest, however, is a protected environment. In their crown shyness, they elegantly leave room for other trees to thrive
- I like fireworks, especially exploding in reverse
- I like thunderstorms and lightning and tame fires
- I live in a perpetual state of longing, but this can occasionally be harnessed as motivation to stretch beyond what currently is (Sehnsucht again)
- I speak several languages that have marvellous words and phrases for unique things, which reminds me that This Is Not All There Is, there are Other Ways of Knowing, and the world is still big enough to get lost in:
- Zerrissenheit: a word in German that describes perfectly my state of inner strife or internal fragmentation (famously translated by the philosopher William James as 'torn-to-pieces-hood');
- Zersetzung: a technique of psychological warfare used very effectively by the Stasi against East German

- political opponents in the 1970s and 1980s, and useful for understanding my married years;
- and then: Quando Dio finisce le ali per gli angeli, mette le code: when God finishes making the wings for angels, he puts tails
- I like to take very hot baths in the dark
- I have an over-developed sense of the absurd, and I really like to laugh

I am trying to begin at the beginning. Sometimes this is an overwhelming idea, and I can only manage the small gift of rapt attention. Soon I hope to manage more.

Sometimes I like to make a liturgy of Beginnings hoping that a) a turning point will reveal itself, the moment Things Could Have Turned Out Differently and b) that a satisfactory continuation — ending even — will present itself. Beginnings are not difficult to spot; endings are more problematic, any writer will tell you that.

It all began with the fire —

It all began with the bird —

It all began with the plant —

It began when my son refused to leave the house —

It began when the police came —

It began when He broke into my phone and my private conversation ceased to —

It began each morning with a liturgy recited of reasons to stay alive —

(the liturgy began with my children)

It began when He refused to leave the house —

It began with Britney Spears —
(He tried to make them fear me.)

I SALLY FORTH INTO the early evening, picnic baskets aloft.

You cannot imprison the stars, you cannot put all the sunlight in a jar. The clouds will not obey your threats, and the butterflies will not be charmed.

(I am attempting to feel free in this un-free moment.)

THE POET: Alice's Cheshire cat understood that you have to vanish into pieces to protect the whole.

I have been doing that for more than a decade; sometimes there is too much vanishment and you forget how to come back. It is one of the dangers of this strategy.

The wind has settled a little, as it does most evenings. I must find a sheltered spot when I get to the park; I have allowed time for a careful search.

And then there he is, cresting the hill in the road, proud paws lifting high.

'Walk with me Bruce,' I call out. 'We can spot the children as they arrive. Which way do you prefer?'

(The pavement is too hot for Bruce's feet! This is why he is picking them up like a dancing horse. I move to the grass.)

BRUCE: I like the un-path best.

(Yes.)

We follow his magnificent nose.

'This evening, Bruce, I want to celebrate the impossibility of Capture, the ultimate impotence of walls and boxes faced with the power of the desire to be free, to grow, to be shaped like coastal trees by the wind, by the inexplicable, by the trust we have to have in the universe itself.'

Downwind now, Bruce catches the scent of the cheese, and he picks up the pace.

'I want to slip and slide over and around the world that is organised to exclude the Living Ones who don't Fit or Matter according to the invisible but oh-so-visible hierarchical organising structure of the society I am surrounded by.'

THE ARCHER: More vexed hierarchies, Winona — when will you learn your place?!

THE NANNY: Some forces when resisted grow stronger —

THE ARCHER: And some forces must be resisted in order for us to become strong! Every conflict is a war over who gets to tell the story and who gets believed —

Bruce looks up at me with those incredible orange eyes.

'I'm sorry for the voices, Bruce. They get very loud sometimes and argumentative. But I tell myself that there was a time past when voices were a Good Thing: mystics, visionaries, poets, prophets, shamans, wise women — it was all very respectable and even revered to Hear Things Unsung and Unseen.'

BRUCE: What are you really trying to say, Winona? You are orbiting the nub of it.

I challenge myself to stop and be true:

'That I understand shame, Bruce. I know it, I understand it, but my knowing does not mean I can erase it. I am a cloth dipped in the indigo of the indignance of others.'

BRUCE: Purple prose — apologies, but the pun is irresistible. However, now I feel we are getting somewhere.

'I am feeling florid, yes. But also ashamed. I feel intense

shame. It is an ugly, hidden feeling. Acknowledging it doesn't make it loosen its grip.'

BRUCE: No. But naming it is taking the un-path. Some forces when resisted grow stronger.

'So I've been told.'

BRUCE: (Perhaps it might be time for shame to switch sides). We walk on.

The wind breaks over us in warm, uneven swells. I spot the pagoda ahead. It will be a good shelter from the wind when it picks up.

Bruce tells me what he has learned about the almost-drowned surfer from sitting like a Good Boy outside the grocer and listening: the man was face-down in the water for eight minutes, with a head-injury sustained either by the rocks or his board. It took the rescuers forty minutes with a defibrillator to start his heart again. But they did. The surfer is in an induced coma, but remarkably and miraculously and against every odd we think we know, his brain has not suffered; he is expected to make a full and complete recovery.

There are photographs of miracles, and this is one.

(I keep the morning's image of body as marionette as further proof of the possibility of Great Reversals, as a talisman and as a story that reminds me I am so very glad to be alive.)

BRUCE: Yes. To make a home inside yourself and to retain a light heart … this is the beginning of winning, Winona.

The hill rises up to meet us, the wind is at our back. I hear them before I see them, little voices. I cry out as they appear in the distance, my hearts. They start running running running towards me, into the wind. Irirangi, the Māori bodyguard in the background, waves, and I wave back, and I am smiling so hard my face wants to split. I kneel and take them both into my open arms and hug and hug and hug. I want to weep, but the time for tears is over. We rise as one, each boy attached to my side, leaning into each other. There can be no crack for anything beyond this present moment to creep in and lodge; nothing must be permitted to wedge there.

The sun is smudging low and red, the clouds strangely purple on either side as if the sun were a bloodshot eye in a boxer's face. This is no sunset — they speak of false dawns, but this is a false twilight: it is smoke bringing darkness so early, ash and dust creating the wounding gash of red along the horizon and under a charcoal sky. We look towards Bruce, who is investigating the remains of someone's chicken picnic.

'Bruce!'

He turns.

BRUCE: I won't be a moment.

'Look!'

He follows my gaze and sees the shadow we cast, the boys and I in our hug. Now we are not three people hugging: we have transformed into something Other and something More; our hug casts upon the heat-blistered grass the shadow of the mother fig. Somehow, the accidental positioning of our bodies, of limbs, has summoned a True Shadow; it has conjured a way for us to understand something more real. Like the wayang puppet, we see our shadowselves; we see what we truly are.

Bruce gets up and lumbers over and sits, adding another trapezius muscle to the shadow-shoulders of our mother tree. He is sitting on the foot of my youngest boy, who reaches out and gently, ever so gently, takes hold of his ears.

We raise our arms now and wave them — we grow swaying branches, allow the wind to move through us.

'Shall we try to walk without letting go of each other and see what happens to our shadow?'

We begin walking, the children still waving — for an instant, we are a giant octopus, a squid, a tangled forest — then we break apart, laughing. This is a good game.

We hold shadow hands in a chain — touching shadow-fingertips and shadow-palms — not touching in real life.

'Look! As we walk side by side — even our shadows love each other!'

My older boy throws heart shapes with his small hands, dark whole hearts in quick succession.

'This is how you could touch someone without touching them — can you feel this?'

I am stroking my youngest boy's shadow arm. He pauses for a moment then nods solemnly.

(*Yes.*)

(*I could put my faith in this.*)

'We are all just walking each other home.' (Ram Dass)

Irirangi stands at our side now, smiling. My boys notice that he casts an important shadow, more mountain than man. He holds his arms wide, then presses his palms on his head and it becomes a fin.

'My name means spirit voice in Māori.'

'Can you sing?' The boys want to know.

'I can sing "Baby Shark" in Māori —'

He starts singing *Pepi Mako* and the boys yell in protest:

'No one wants that tune stuck in their heads!'

We are all laughing now.

THE POET: Just keep the joy flowing; nothing else is permitted. Beam LOVE as if your life depended on it. Summon every intergalactic particle you have ever swallowed and feed your children this cosmic force, weave an enchantment, transmit your heart by whatever means necessary, bleed to death if you must, like the pelican mother who opened her own artery to feed her starving babies ...

I set out a patterned cloth and begin placing olives and carrots and rice crackers safely out of the wind.

'Today it's a picnic dinner!'

The boys will not leave my side, but it becomes a game; we move as one beast.

Irirangi is holding a clipboard to make notes on my mothering; we are all ignoring this, including him. He accepts an olive.

'You are a very good mother, Winona.' (He says this quietly, as if it were a secret which perhaps it is.) 'You're a really great mum.'

THE ARCHER: Don't let that in either, let it slide over you like the wind, smile, your gratitude is in your face, thank and move on. It is desperately unsafe to dwell on how you ended up in a park with a large Māori man overseeing your mothering and —

Stop. Just stop.

THE POET: (What you omit sometimes says more than the things you include. The silence will be your offering — words make silence possible.)

But I broke the silence! An unhappy family is always a conspiracy of silence, and I stopped being complicit in it. I can never be forgiven that.

The wind is picking up, and some rice crackers take flight. We watch them flip and tumble unevenly along the ground. The wind can only be seen in our imagination, its restlessness felt on our skin, in our hair, our fur, our leaves — the sound that feels like the faraway breath of the very earth on strong days — and yet we can only ever see its consequence, never the wind itself.

Breeze is gusting its way to gale and soon we will have to seek shelter. I lift the cloth and it billows like a mad sail.

No feeling is final.

BRUCE: What now for you?

I stand and absorb the strength of the wind.

THE CHILD: What will happen tomorrow? And tomorrow? And tomorrow ...?

'Let them think I am a tree.'

I stretch on my tippy toes, still holding the sail canopy aloft. It whips and cracks in the wind. The boys stretch with me, and we grow even taller as the sun sinks; we sway our uppermost branches, our shadow sliding out across the grass; then we turn to face that crimson sun, and our shadow vanishes in an apocalypse of light.

ACKNOWLEDGEMENTS

THANK YOU TO GRACE HEIFETZ at A4 literary agency, and to John Ash at CAA London. Thank you to my editor and publisher, Marika Webb-Pullman, whose talent and sensitivity is a dream to work with, and to the amazing team at Scribe, both in Australia and the UK: Sophia Benjamin, Tina Gumnior, Chris Grierson, Alice Richardson, and Adam Howard. Winona is very fortunate to have your talents propelling her story. Thanks to Duncan Blachford for the text design. Luke Bird, your cover designs are inspired — thank you!

My ecosystem is sustained by many beautiful, generous humans, and more-than-humans: you know who you are and how grateful I am. A special grazie to Dado, whose furry ever-presence accompanies me always as I write.